In this exciting new duet by
Scarlet Wilson

discover these

Tycoons in a Million
Romance in a rich man's world...

Friends Reuben Tyler and Caleb Connor have
chosen very different paths in life. Caleb
married his sweetheart whilst Reuben played
the field, but they both climbed to
the dizzying heights of success!

Now, with the world at their fingertips,
these millionaires can have anything
they want. But when it comes to love
Reuben and Caleb realise there are
some things money can't buy...

The Connors' nanny Lara Callaway is a
breath of fresh air for rebellious Reuben in

Holiday with the Millionaire
Available now!

And can the Connors save their
seemingly perfect marriage?

Find out in Caleb and Addison's story...
Coming soon!

Dear Reader,

This is the first story in my duet about two friends: Reuben Tyler and Caleb Connor.

Reuben is my original bad boy—a sports agent with a delicious Irish accent and film star looks. Every time you read about Reuben think Colin Farrell—he was in my head the whole time I was writing this story! Reuben's about to meet the perfect woman to show him what love is—he just doesn't know it yet.

Lara Callaway has had a jumble of jobs and has finally ended up as nanny to Addison and Caleb Connor's son. She's been saving for her dream holiday—a cruise— for months, and is just about to jet off when she has her own *Sliding Doors* moment when she gets an earlier tube home and finds her boyfriend in bed with someone else.

With one loser boyfriend after another she's determined not to make the same mistake again. That *Sliding Doors* moment leaves her with nowhere to stay just before her holiday, and she has to ask Addison if she can stay temporarily at her house. The trouble is Caleb has also told his friend Reuben Tyler *he* can stay, and when the pair finally meet sparks fly—mainly because Lara thinks he's a burglar and hits him over the head!

I loved writing about this duo, with Reuben introducing Lara to a world of glamour and prestige. How could any girl possibly resist?

Thanks for reading!

Scarlet Wilson

PS I love to hear from readers—contact me via my website: scarlet-wilson.com.

HOLIDAY WITH THE MILLIONAIRE

BY
SCARLET WILSON

MILLS
BOON

First published in Great Britain 2016
by Mills & Boon, an imprint of Harlequin (UK) Limited,
Eton House, 18-24 Paradise Road, Richmond, Surrey, TW9 1SR

© 2016 Scarlet Wilson

ISBN: 978-0-263-26341-1

Scarlet Wilson writes for both Mills & Boon Romance and Medical Romance. She lives on the west coast of Scotland with her fiancé and their two sons. She loves to hear from readers and can be reached via her website: scarlet-wilson.com.

Visit the Author Profile page at
millsandboon.co.uk for more titles.

This book is dedicated to my auntie, Margaret Wilson, and my honorary auntie, Mary Hamilton. Doris and Daisy with their holiday antics are based on you two!

CHAPTER ONE

LARA TRIED TO hide her sniffles as the door opened and Addison's chin nearly hit the perfect hardwood flooring.

'Lara? What on earth...?'

She didn't wait for her to finish. Rain was dripping off the end of her nose and running down her back as she tried to bump her impossibly heavy case over the entranceway of the house. The case gave a squeak and one of the wheels catapulted merrily into the air, spinning off down the front steps and along the exclusive London street.

She swallowed the impossible lump in her throat. It pretty much summed up her life right now.

Addison pulled her by the elbow and slammed the door behind her. 'What's wrong? What's happened?'

Lara's stomach coiled up. She hated this. She hated turning up like this. Even though she tried to hide it, she knew Addison was stressed enough without adding anything else into the mix. Her pretty face had been marred by a permanent frown for the last few months Lara had been acting as a nanny for her and her husband, Caleb.

She took a deep breath. She was still in shock and the words just seemed to come out of nowhere. 'I had a *Sliding Doors* moment,' she breathed, before dissolving into tears.

'A what?' The frown was back. Addison had no idea what she was talking about.

Lara shook her head, her blonde hair sending raindrops splattering all around them. 'I went home earlier than he expected. I caught the earlier tube.' Her voice wobbled.

Addison took a deep breath and stood up a little taller. 'And?' She could be scary when she wanted to be.

'And Josh was in bed with the next-door neighbour.'

She wobbled and Addison caught hold of her elbow and steered her through to the kitchen. 'I'm sorry, Addison. I know you're just about to go on holiday but I had nowhere else to go. I just stuffed everything into my case and left.'

Addison flicked the switch on the coffee machine. 'That ratbag. How dare he? You've paid the rent on that flat for—how long? And he does this to you?'

She opened the cupboard and pulled out two cups then sat down on the stool opposite Lara. 'What are you going to do?'

Lara hesitated. The timing was, oh, so wrong. 'I'm sorry, Addison. I know you're leaving in the next few hours. This is the last thing you need.' It was the absolute last thing. Although to outsiders Addison and Caleb Connor had the perfect life, Lara could tell that things were strained. Their son, Tristan, was a dream to nanny, a happy, well-mannered little boy with the biggest smile in the world. But things in the household were far from happy. Addison had been strangely silent these last few weeks, and Caleb's presence had been virtually non-existent. Lara had the distinct impression this month-long holiday was make or break for the couple.

She bit her lip. 'I wondered...can I stay for the next couple of weeks? Just until I try and sort things out? I'll need to find somewhere else to stay.'

Addison didn't hesitate. 'Of course you can. No problem at all. Caleb and I will be gone in the next few hours. You can have the place to yourself and take some time to get sorted.'

She pressed some buttons on the state-of-the-art coffee machine. She frowned at Lara, 'Double shot?'

Lara nodded. Addison pressed a few more buttons for

the extra shot for Lara and decaf for herself and the steaming hot lattes appeared in seconds. She held up two syrup bottles. 'Gingerbread or caramel?'

'Vodka,' Lara groaned. It might only be three o'clock in the afternoon but after the day she'd had she wanted to cut straight to the chase. She pointed over at the one in Addison's left hand. 'Caramel.'

Addison poured a healthy amount of pure sugar syrup into the latte before adding the tiniest dash into her own.

She looked Lara straight in the eye. 'What are you going to do about your holiday?'

The holiday. Of course. Lara pressed her head down on the counter worktop. 'Oh, no.'

Addison reached over and squeezed her hand. 'You've been looking forward to this all year. Don't let him spoil this for you. You deserve a holiday. You need a holiday. Spend the next two weeks sorting yourself out, then go and lie in the sun. Relax. Chill out.'

'By myself?' The holiday she'd been looking forward to for months had instantly lost its shine. There was something really wrong about going on a cruise on your own. Talk about awkward.

Addison's glare had a steely edge. 'Yes, by yourself. Why not? You don't need a man to determine who you are in this life. You've saved hard for that holiday. Go and enjoy it.' She picked up her latte. 'Now, I need to finish packing. Will you be okay?'

Lara shifted on the stool. She really needed to get out of these rain-soaked clothes. Her stomach was churning. She could sense the tension in the air around Addison. It wasn't like her to say something so direct. She usually kept all her cards played safely close to her chest. Still, it wasn't her place to say anything. The line between employer and employee still existed and she shouldn't cross it. Her only concern should be Tristan, and from all her observations he was a happy, healthy little boy. Whatever was going on between the adults was up to them to solve.

She nodded her head in grateful relief. 'I'm not right now, but I will be. Thanks, Addison. I promise I'll take good care of the place.'

'I know you will,' Addison replied, with the quiet reassurance she always possessed. She paused for a second, 'I won't be able to call or email you. The place we're going—it doesn't have a phone line or internet.' She paused and gave a sad kind of smile. 'You'll be fine, Lara. You don't need him. He didn't deserve you—not at all. It's amazing how strong you can be on your own when you need to be.' She held Lara's gaze. 'The world needs good people like you. Look after yourself.' She gave a nod of her head and disappeared out into the hall.

Lara sucked in a deep breath, looked around the immaculate show kitchen and put her head back on the counter.

Two weeks to sort herself out. Perfect.

It was almost midnight. Reuben fumbled with the key in the lock yet again and swore under his breath.

Maybe he shouldn't have had that extra drink but his flight had been delayed six hours, jet-lag was kicking in and he'd decided to stop to try and get something to eat before he got back to the house.

Only something to eat had turned into something to drink. The takeaway hadn't looked too appetising and the pub across the road had stopped serving food at seven p.m. So he'd just had a drink. That had turned into another. And then another. Watching a football match in a pub had that effect. After five minutes everyone was your best friend.

The key finally clicked into place and he shouldered the door open, falling over the front step and landing in a heap on the hardwood floor. The entrance hall was so big the noise echoed around him.

He picked himself up and tried to feel his way along the wall, seeking a light switch. When was the last time he'd been in Caleb's house? Must have been over a year ago—Addison wasn't exactly welcoming. She didn't seem to like her husband's bad-boy friend.

The light switch wasn't beckoning. All he felt was the flat walls. His eyes tried to adjust to the dark. If he remembered correctly the kitchen was to the right and the living room to the left, looking out over the exclusive London street.

He sighed and headed towards the living room. He'd collapse on the sofa and watch TV for a bit.

He froze in mid-step. What was that? Was that a noise?

He held his breath for a second. Caleb, Addison and their son should be on holiday. Caleb had said he could stay here for the next few weeks while his house was getting roof repairs. He tipped his head to the side and listened again.

No. Nothing.

He dumped his bag at his feet and walked over to the outline of the door to the living room and pushed it open. All he really wanted to do right now was sprawl out on the sofa.

But everything was wrong. And the jet-lag meant that all the senses in his brain were firing in slow-mo.

If he'd been firing on all cylinders he would have noticed immediately the glowing television on the wall, the sweet wrappers and wine bottle on the living-room table and the duvet on the sofa. *His sofa.*

Instead, all he noticed was the flash in the corner of his eye and the thudding pain at the back of his head. As he made contact with the floor and looked upwards all he could see was something pink and fuzzy.

Then everything went black.

* * *

She couldn't breathe. There was a tight strap across her chest and her heart was thudding wildly in her ears.

One minute she'd been lying half-dozing on the sofa, watching Saturday night TV, the next she'd heard footsteps walking across the entranceway. She'd gone into autopilot—years of watching too many TV shows—and picked up the nearest thing to hand. It was one of Caleb's awards and it was currently lying broken on the floor next to the burglar in black.

She picked up the phone and dialled the police. 'Emergency services. Which service do you require?'

'Police.'

'Police, how can we help you?'

'There's a burglar. In my house. I've hit him.'

'What's your name?'

'Lara. Lara Callaway.'

'Can you give me your address, Lara?'

'Seventeen Crawford Square, Belgravia.'

'Where is the suspect now, Lara?'

She gulped. 'At my feet.' Police, she'd asked for the police. Maybe she should have asked for an ambulance?

'Lara, what do you mean, the suspect is at your feet? Are you in any danger?'

Her mouth was suddenly dry. Maybe she shouldn't have drunk all that wine? 'No. I don't think so. He's unconscious. I hit him.'

The operator spoke slowly. 'Without putting yourself in any danger, can I ask you to check that he's breathing? I'm adding an ambulance to the dispatch call.'

Lara bent her knees and squinted at the guy on the floor. He was lit only by the TV glowing on the far wall. His chest was rising and falling slowly.

She took a deep breath. For a man who was breaking into people's homes he was actually very handsome. He didn't have that furtive, shady look about him. There was a hint of suntan under the shadow along his jawline. He gave a little groan and she jumped back.

'Yes, yes, he's breathing. But I think he's going to wake up.'

'Lara, take yourself to a safe place. The police are on their way and will be at your address in under two minutes. Keep this phone with you. You can keep talking to me if you're scared.'

She backed off out of the room and headed to the front door. Her head was starting to throb. This was turning into a nightmare.

Maybe this was her fault. This was a prestigious London address—of course they would be at risk of housebreaking. The house had a state-of-the-art alarm system—which she hadn't put on yet. She would have done on her way to bed. She just hadn't got that far yet.

Something struck her as strange. How had the burglar got in? The front door was still closed. None of the windows seemed open. What if he'd damaged the house somewhere? Through the window the glow of blue lights in the distance made her breathe a sigh of relief.

How was she going to explain this to Addison?

This was the worst jet-lag *ever.*

'Sir, can you open your eyes for me, please?'

And why was this bed so hard?

'Sir?'

'Yeow!' Someone had nipped the soft flesh on his hand. He sat bolt upright, ignoring the pounding headache.

Wow. He swayed. Dizzy. That was a new experience for him. He hadn't been dizzy since that time he'd been knocked out while playing football ten years ago.

Knocked out. He narrowed his gaze as the pieces started to fall into place. Two policemen. Two green-suited paramedics—one male, one female. And another female dressed in a pink fuzzy pyjama suit with her blonde hair in some kind of weird bundle on top of her head. She looked like some kind of giant kid's toy.

He lifted his hand to the back of his head and winced. 'Someone want to tell me what on earth is going on here?' He frowned and turned to face the pink teddy bear. 'And who the hell are you?'

The teddy-bear face looked indignant. He could tell she was trying to place his Irish accent, which got thicker the angrier he was. 'Who am I? Who are you? You broke into my house!'

One of the policemen stepped forward but Reuben held up his hand. 'Wait a minute—you're not Addison. This isn't *your* house.'

He stood up and dusted himself off. 'And I didn't break in anywhere. I have a key…' he pulled it from his back pocket '…because I am supposed to be staying here. So who are you exactly?'

The policeman looked from one to the other. 'It would probably help if you could both identify who you are.'

The paramedic stepped forward. 'I'm not finished yet.' She held up a penlight and shone it into Reuben's eyes. He flinched but didn't object. He knew better. After a second she gave a nod. 'Both pupils equal and reactive.' She stepped back to write some notes.

Reuben pulled his wallet out from his back pocket and handed it to one of the policemen. 'Reuben Tyler. I just landed from LA a few hours ago.' He folded his arms across his chest. 'My own apartment is under repair. It took damage during the recent storm and when they went to do repairs they discovered asbestos in the roof.' He turned to glare at the teddy bear again. She really was quite cute. If he hadn't been having such a bad day he might have been quite taken by her strange get-up, perfect skin and mussed-up hair. 'My friend Caleb Connor, who owns this place, said I could stay here while he and his family were on holiday.'

The policeman turned towards the teddy bear, who was shifting uncomfortably on her feet at the mention of Caleb's name. 'And you are?'

'I'm Lara Callaway. I work for the Connors. I'm their nanny.'

Ah, their nanny. Things were starting to fall into place in his brain. Caleb had said the last nanny had left and they'd hired someone new.

'And I can verify this with the Connors?'

He watched as she gulped and glanced at the clock. This was a girl who obviously wasn't used to being around the police.

'Well...not right now. They'll be midway across the Atlantic—and they're going to a place with no phone or internet.' She turned around to look at Reuben. 'You're not going to take him at his word, are you? I've never seen him before—and I've never heard Mr Connor mention his name. He could be anyone.'

Reuben rolled his eyes and sighed. The teddy bear was starting to get annoying. He glanced about the living room, his eyes fixing on a distant photo frame. He stalked across the room and picked it up, thrusting it towards the policeman while glaring at Lara. 'Here, photographic evidence. That's me and Caleb at an awards ceremony around five years ago. And...' he pulled his phone from his pocket '...here's a text from Caleb, telling me how to switch off his alarm.'

He ran his eyes up and down Lara's fuzzy-covered frame. She might be wearing the most unsexy nightwear in the world but it still gave a hint of her curves. She wiggled her pink painted toes as if she could sense his gaze on her. 'And as for the nanny...' he gestured with his head towards her '…I've never heard of her. According to Caleb, I would be the only one staying here.' He gave a little laugh. 'As for no phone and no internet? I'll bet Caleb didn't know that before he left. He might be on the other side of the Atlantic but I'm pretty sure we'll hear him blow up from here.'

All he really wanted to do was get his head down—and maybe find something to eat. His head ached and he couldn't believe the commotion. So much for some quiet downtime.

Lara looked flustered by his words. 'I've worked for the family for the last six months. The nanny before me left. Addison—Mrs Connor—said I could stay here for the next couple of weeks. I've had a bit of a…misunderstanding and she agreed at short notice.'

Reuben's ears pricked up at her words and he couldn't stop a smile appearing on his face. She was obviously easily flustered, not used to being around the police and feeling distinctly uneasy. Then again, she was in her nightwear—even if it did cover every part of her body—and it was obvious she'd decided to have feast in front of the TV. Probably not the scene you wanted all these people to see.

'What was the misunderstanding?' he pressed. He was amused now. 'The one that made you hit me over the head with something.'

He looked around the floor to see what she'd hit him with and saw the remains of something on the floor. He bent down and picked up the broken marble and gold trophy. His mouth fell open. 'You hit me with the Businessman of the Year award? Oh, wow, Caleb will be *mad*.' He pointed over to the photo of Caleb and himself, showing Caleb clearly holding up the award with pride.

If she'd been flustered before she looked positively pained now. 'But I didn't know who you were. And I thought you were a burglar. I thought you were going to attack me.' Her voice started to wobble and her eyes started to fill. 'I didn't know what to do.'

The policeman put a hand on her arm. 'We understand, but Mr Tyler does have a right to press charges.'

'Charges?' She could barely get the word out and he could see her start to shake.

'For assault.'

She wobbled. She looked as if her legs were going to give out completely.

Enough. He needed this to be over with.

'There won't be any charges. Not from me anyway. I'm sure Ms Callaway will be able to speak to Caleb about replacing his award.' He looked towards the other policeman, who'd been talking quietly into his radio. 'Have you verified us yet? Can we finish this?'

The paramedic raised her eyebrows at him. 'Actually, no, we can't. You were knocked out, Mr Tyler. We should really take you to hospital to be checked over.'

'No. No. I definitely don't want to do that.'

But as he shook his head he realised how dizzy he was. It was all he could do not to sway. He eyed the sofa for a second, wondering if he should sit down.

'We're obliged to take you, Mr Tyler. There can be serious repercussions from a head injury. It will only take a few hours.'

'In London on a Saturday night? You've got to be joking. Every A and E around here will have queues out the door.' He waved his hand. 'I'm fine.'

The paramedic frowned and her lips thinned. This woman was formidable. It was time to take a different tack.

'Look, I've just got off a long flight from the US and I'm tired. I just want to find something to eat and get to sleep. I haven't slept in the last thirty-six hours. You said my pupils were equal, surely that means I'm okay?'

She hesitated and glanced at her partner. 'After a head injury some symptoms take a while to appear. You might feel okay now, but in a few hours it could be different.'

The policemen were exchanging glances. The only person in the room who couldn't look at him was Lara—the giant teddy bear.

'I really don't want to go to hospital,' he said steadily.

The paramedic glanced from him to Lara. 'Well, I'll have to get you to sign something. Then I'll give you a final check and leave some head-injury instructions. You can't be left alone. There needs to be someone around you in case you feel unwell later and need to go to hospital.'

A smile broke across his face. 'Oh, I'm sure Ms Callaway will oblige.'

Her head shot up. 'What? Me? No!' She turned towards the policeman. 'You're not actually going to let him stay here, are you? I don't know him. I don't want to be left in a house with a stranger.' Her indignation made him smile even more.

The policeman looked at her. 'Then perhaps you'd like to stay somewhere else? You did say you made this arrangement at short notice. Maybe there's somewhere else you can stay?'

She cringed. 'What? No.' She was starting to look a bit panicked. But there was no way at this late stage that Reuben was going to ring around friends to find a bed for the night. He'd made this arrangement with Caleb and he was sticking to it—whether Ms Teddy Bear liked it or not.

The paramedic stood in front of Reuben. 'Can you sit down for a second while I do some final checks?'

She couldn't possibly know how grateful he was to sink down onto the comfortable overstuffed sofa. His stomach gave a little growl as he noticed all the sweet papers on the coffee table. The smell of chocolate and cheese and onion crisps was drifting in his direction. He didn't care who it belonged to. As soon as he got rid of these folks he was eating the entire lot.

A paramedic made a few final notes and handed him a clipboard and pen. 'Sign here.'

He scribbled his name and took the leaflet she proffered. She gave him a suspicious glance as she stood up. 'If you have any of the symptoms on the card you must attend the nearest A and E.' She gestured with her head. 'It's St David's, about a mile in that direction.'

He gave her a nod. 'Thanks.'

The policemen headed towards the door. 'We'll file a report but I take it things are settled now?'

Lara stood with her mouth gaping. She looked shell-shocked. 'But—'

'I'm sure everything will be fine,' the other policeman cut in. 'Goodnight, Ms Callaway, Mr Tyler,' he said, as all four people filed out the front door.

Reuben stood again, waiting for them all to leave before finally closing the front door behind them. His legs felt heavy, but nowhere near as heavy as the thudding in his head.

He stalked back through to the sitting room, collapsed on the couch and tore open one of the chocolate bars, grabbing the TV remote.

Lara hadn't moved. She was still rooted to the spot.

He grinned at her wickedly. 'Well, then, I guess it's just you and me.'

CHAPTER TWO

THIS COULDN'T BE HAPPENING.

An hour ago she'd been watching one of her favourite eighties movies as she'd sipped wine and eaten her body weight in chocolates.

Now it felt as if the Terminator had just invaded her comfortable living space. Except this terminator had an Irish accent that was almost musical to her ears.

Not that Reuben Tyler looked like Arnie. And with his black jeans and leather jacket he was maybe a little too stylish for a burglar. She was trying not to stare. She was trying not to look at him at all. What on earth was she going to do?

'So, do you always dress like a giant teddy bear?' he said as he flicked through the channels.

'What?' She stared down at her favourite nightwear. Oh, no. In all the chaos she'd forgotten how she was dressed. Hardly a good look for a first meeting.

She scowled at him and stuck her hands on her hips. 'Well, it wasn't like I was expecting guests, was I?'

The corner of his mouth turned upwards. 'Evidently.'

Okay, this guy could make her blood boil but was he a tiny bit hunky? She stole another glance. When he wasn't angry, he might be described as quite handsome in a rugged sort of way. His dark hair was thick and a little dishevelled. His white T-shirt showed off his tan—doubtless from his stay in the US since it had rained solidly for the last month in London. No wonder she was keeping her pale flesh covered. But it was those eyes that could probably melt the hearts of the female population of the city. Dark brown, like coffee or chocolate—both were her vices.

She gave a little shudder. What on earth was she thinking? She didn't know a single thing about this man.

'You can't possibly stay here. Addison told me I'd have the place to myself for the next few days.' She folded her arms across her chest. She was grasping at straws but Addison really hadn't mentioned a word about having to share the place with one of Caleb's friends. Which most likely meant that Addison hadn't known that Reuben would be here...

Darn it. There went the little shudder again. All of a sudden he wasn't so much a dangerous intruder as a slightly intriguing handsome stranger. But sharing the house with someone she didn't know still made her feel uncomfortable.

Reuben seemed completely uninterested in her comments. He grabbed a bar of chocolate from the table and started eating it. 'I think you should be more worried about smashing up Caleb's trophy. He was very proud of that.'

The trophy. Her eyes went to the floor. It was broken into three solid parts. No super-strength glue in the world could put it back together. She sagged down into one of the armchairs. 'I've no idea what to do about that,' she murmured.

Reuben sat up a little straighter. He gave his head a little shake and winced. 'Do you have any painkillers?'

She nodded. 'Come through to the kitchen. There are some in the cupboard.'

She flashed her hand over the light for the hall and it came on, flooding the entranceway with light. Reuben frowned and bent down. 'What on earth is that? I couldn't find the light switch when I came in.'

She walked past. 'It's one of Caleb's new inventions.

Light switches you don't touch. Just the motion of your hand switches it on. Do you know that light switches and doorhandles are the biggest places that harbour germs?'

She couldn't believe she was having a normal conversation with a guy she'd thought was breaking into the house. It was all so surreal. Maybe this was a dream? Maybe she'd drunk a little too much wine and fallen asleep in front of the TV? Because, truth be told, Reuben Tyler did look a little like a dream.

She stubbed her toe on the way into the kitchen. 'Youch!' She definitely wasn't dreaming. That had hurt too much.

She waved her hand over the switch to turn the light on and walked to the cupboard on the far wall to retrieve the tablets. Reuben sat on one of the stools at the kitchen island and gave a little sigh.

She grabbed a glass and filled it with water. 'Here you go.' She hesitated then added, 'I'm sorry about your head.'

He looked up at her through lazy, tired eyes. 'Yeah, yeah. I'm sure I'll get over it.'

He was looking at her with those chocolate eyes. The stare was so intense it almost felt as if it was burrowing through her thick pink onesie. It was *definitely* heading for the bin after this. His gaze made her feel uneasy and she started to ramble. 'There are a few free bedrooms upstairs. I'm on the second floor so I'd appreciate it if you could sleep on one of the other floors. Maybe the third? Since Addison, Caleb and Tristan all sleep on the first floor.'

'You're pushing me into the servants' quarters?' His voice was a lazy drawl.

'What? I am not.'

'Yes, you are. Don't you remember that in all these Georgian houses the servants stayed in the attics?'

'Did they?' She wrinkled her nose. 'I wasn't much of

a history buff, more a geography girl myself.' She waved her hand. 'Anyway the rooms upstairs are lovely. The biggest one has an en-suite bathroom, I'm sure you'll be comfortable there.'

He was still watching her, almost as if he was trying to size her up. But what alarmed her most was the fact there was a twinkle in his eye. He swallowed the painkillers and took a gulp of the water. 'Maybe I'll just crash on the sofa—next to your midnight feast. Were you actually going to eat all that?'

Colour heated her cheeks. She was about to be offended, but from the twinkle in his eye it was almost as if he was trying to bait her. She'd recovered enough from the shock of earlier to play him at his own game.

'I was going to eat all that. And you owe me. Don't think I didn't notice that you swiped one of my favourite chocolate bars.' She wagged her finger at him. 'Touch anything else and I'll give you more than a sore head.'

He surprised her. He threw back his head and laughed, just as his stomach growled loudly. He shrugged his shoulders. 'What can I say? I'm starving.' He stood up and started prowling around the kitchen, staring at the uniform white cupboards as if he didn't know which to open first. 'Is there anything to eat around here?'

Lara watched him for a few seconds. That was definitely a pair of well-fitting jeans. They hugged every inch of his thighs and backside, even though she could see the waist was a little loose. His white T-shirt was rumpled and there was tiny hint of curling dark hairs and flat abs. It was all she could do to tear her eyes away.

She sighed. 'As I was a late arrival too and Addison had run down most of the fresh food, there's only what I bought tonight.' She opened the fridge. 'I have bread, bacon and baked beans.'

He was smiling again and counted off on his fingers,

'And wine, and chocolate, and crisps, and some kind of cake I didn't even recognise.'

She smiled and shook her head. 'Don't even think about it—all of those are out of bounds.'

He leaned against one of the cupboards. 'Well, I've thought about it. I know how you can make it up to me.'

'Make what up to you?'

'The fact you assaulted me with one of Caleb's trophies.' He put his hand on his chin. 'I'm thinking a bacon-and-baked-bean sandwich might just cut it.'

'You don't put bacon and baked beans in a sandwich.' She shook her head in disgust. 'Especially not at one in the morning.'

The glint remained in his eyes as they swept up and down her body and he lifted his hand to his head. 'Ouch.' He gave the back of his head an exaggerated rub. 'I think one o'clock in the morning sounds a perfect time for a bacon-and-baked-bean sandwich. Hours past dinner and hours until breakfast.'

She pursed her lips. He was getting to her. He was definitely getting to her. She wasn't quite sure if it was the guilt trip working or the rising tension she could feel in the air between them.

'Fine.' She turned around and flicked a few switches on the coffee machine. 'What do you want to drink?'

He stared at the machine as his brow creased. She hid her smile. The first time she'd seen the coffee machine she had been bamboozled by it. It had taken a few attempts to finally get it right.

'What does that do—make coffee or beam you up?'

'Oh, if it could beam you up I'd press that button right away,' she said smartly, as she walked back over to the fridge, pulled out the bacon and fired up the grill.

He folded his arms across his chest. He looked amused,

maybe even intrigued by her sparky response. 'So, now we're getting to see the true you.'

'As opposed to what?'

He laughed. 'As opposed to the crazy ammunition-wielding giant pink teddy bear I met when I arrived.'

She glared at him as she put the bacon under the grill. 'Let's see.' She counted off on her fingers. 'You've ruined my night. It seems like you're going to interrupt the two weeks of sanctuary I was expecting to have here. You've insulted my favourite nightwear. Scared me half to death. Stolen my chocolate and blackmailed me into making you something to eat.' She folded her arms back at him. 'Why, Reuben, you're my favourite person in the world right now.'

He shook his head at her tone. 'I hope you're not serious.'

She opened the cupboard and pulled out a tin of baked beans. 'About which part?'

His cheeky smile reached from ear to ear. 'About the favourite nightwear part. I'm hoping you've got something much more appropriate than that.'

Had he really just said that? He must have because tiny electric sparks were currently shooting down her spine and making her toes curl.

She opened the tin of beans, poured them into a bowl and started to nuke them in the microwave. 'Why do I think you're going to be a pain in the neck to have around?'

He raised his eyebrows. 'You seem to have been hit with a sass attack. Exactly how much wine did you drink?'

'Obviously not enough.'

'Wow.' Reuben mocked being hit in the chest and fell against the wall. 'What's happened to you?'

She shrugged. 'I had an adrenaline surge when I thought someone was breaking in. You know, the old fight-or-flight thing. Then when the police arrived I started to panic.' She turned the bacon over in the grill pan. 'Both those things have left me now. It's late. I planned on being asleep around an hour ago. Instead, I'm playing hostess in a kitchen that isn't mine and plotting an elaborate lie to tell Caleb about his award.'

She stuck some bread in the toaster and walked back over to the coffee machine. 'Now, pick your poison or learn how to work this yourself.'

He laughed and walked over next to her. 'You know, the giant pink teddy bear is losing her appeal.'

'That's fine. I never wanted to be a cuddly toy.' She pressed some buttons and coffee and milk steamed out of the coffee maker.

'I'll have what you're having,' he said quickly. He obviously didn't want to miss out on the chance of coffee and would drink anything.

She made another latte, put the bacon on a plate on the middle of the kitchen island and lifted the steaming-hot bowl of baked beans from the microwave. The toast popped and she took the butter from the fridge and put everything down in front of him, handing him a plate and some cutlery and sitting at the other side of the island.

She could feel the intense brown eyes on her again. Part of her wondered what he was thinking. Part of her was too scared to even think that far.

He started buttering his toast. 'I thought I asked for a sandwich.' He kept buttering.

She could feel her anger starting to smart. This guy was a royal pain in the neck. The tranquil time she'd expected to get here had been ruined. Two weeks to get her head together and make some plans for when she came back from her holidays—hopefully enough time to secure another tenancy somewhere.

'I made an executive decision. Bread would be too squishy.'

The edges of his mouth turned upwards. He was trying to keep a straight face. He lifted the bacon onto his toast and grabbed a spoon for the beans. 'Squishy.'

'Squishy,' she said again as she put her bacon in the middle of her toast and spooned some beans onto the side of her plate.

She lifted the toast towards her mouth. 'Now I'm going to watch you eating that without getting beans all down the front of your white T-shirt.'

'That sounds like a challenge.'

'You bet it is.'

Things were beyond odd. He was beginning to like the pink teddy bear more and more—particularly now she was showing some added spark.

He could tell his mere presence annoyed her. Under normal circumstances he'd probably feel the same way. When Caleb had offered him somewhere to stay while his building work was done he'd been relieved. It wasn't as if he didn't have enough money to check into a hotel—he could have done that easily. But then he would have been constantly around people when what he really wanted was some peace and quiet in order to negotiate a deal with a troublesome sports star.

Even though Addison didn't really approve of him, his days of being a bad boy were more or less over. He just didn't have enough hours in the day any more.

He watched as Lara poked at her plate with a fork, trying to spear the baked beans individually.

'Slippery little suckers,' he said as he tried to hold his sandwich together. She glared at him as he took a bite. After a few seconds he spoke again. 'Okay, you got me. I'll admit it. It tastes great.'

She gave a hint of a smile. 'It is pretty good.'

'Better than chocolate and wine?'

'Never.'

This girl was fun. Or she could be fun if she'd just let her guard down a little.

'So, how did come to be working for Caleb and Addison?'

She sat back on her stool at little and sipped her coffee. 'I met Addison through a mutual friend. She was looking for a nanny at short notice and I had just got back from Australia.'

'What were you doing out there?'

She gave a little shrug. 'I went to see the world but ended up only seeing Perth. I met someone when I got there and ended up working as a nanny for a family there for nearly ten months.'

'Why did you come back?'

She rolled her eyes. 'My visa was going to expire and I hadn't met an Australian I could con into marrying me.'

The more she shot at him the more he liked her. 'I don't believe that for a second.'

She shook her head. 'The guy I met, Josh, was English. Let's just say I don't have a good record with guys. If he's a loser, I'm attracted to him. If he's a cheat, I can't spot it. If he's bad for me in any way, shape or form I seem to fall for him hook, line and sinker.'

Now he was definitely curious. 'You staying here—is this about a guy?'

She let out a sigh. 'Let's just say after today's *Sliding Doors* moment it looks like I'm going my dream holiday on my own.'

'*Sliding Doors?*'

'Yes, as in the movie.'

'Never seen it. What do you mean?'

'You've never seen it?' She shook her head. 'Where have you been? The girl gets out of work early and runs to catch the tube. In one version she makes the train, in the other she doesn't. In the version when she gets home early, she catches her boyfriend in bed with someone else.'

He sat back, bacon and beans forgotten. 'And that happened to you?' Maybe he should actually start watching these chick-flick movies.

She sighed again and nodded.

'Ouch. Blooming fool. Who is he? Do you want me to go and sort him out?'

Her head shot up. She looked surprised. 'Of course I don't.'

He shook his head. 'Oh, please. Don't tell me you still love the guy?'

She leaned her head on her hands. 'I'm not sure I ever really did. I just feel as if I've got "Mug" stamped across my forehead in big letters. I just shoved everything I could into a case and left.'

'How long did you stay together?'

'In London? Just the last six months. I met him when I went travelling to Australia and we rented the flat together when we came back.' She toyed with her coffee cup. 'Not that he actually paid any rent. He was…' she lifted her fingers in the air '"…writing" apparently. I guess that wasn't all he was doing.'

Reuben frowned. 'And who was the other woman?'

She groaned. 'The next-door neighbour. I couldn't even punch her. She's built like an Amazon and could probably squash me beneath one of her size-eight feet.'

He couldn't help it. He let out a laugh.

She picked up the dishtowel and flicked it at him. 'It's not funny!' His coffee cup tipped and few dark brown splashes splattered his white shirt.

He looked down. He'd been travelling for hours and was feeling grubby anyway. Perfect time to change.

He shook his head and started laughing as he undid the buttons. 'Tell me there's a washing machine around here somewhere?' Every white kitchen door looked identical. He had no idea what lay behind any one of them.

Lara had started to laugh but it seemed to die somewhere in her throat. He looked up to see what was wrong. Her eyes were fixed firmly on his chest. It was an automatic reaction. He sucked in his abs—even though he had no need to. He hadn't even thought twice about taking off his shirt. Maybe she was shyer than he'd thought?

'Give me a second till I grab a T-shirt,' he said quickly, walking back out and getting his bag from the hall. He rummaged around and grabbed a black T-shirt, pulling it over his head as he walked back in. 'Now...' he smiled '...where were we?'

Lara hadn't moved. It was as if the words were stuck somewhere at the back of her throat. She gave a little shudder and fixed him with her eyes.

Her very blue eyes.

He hadn't been paying enough attention.

He'd already noticed the hint of curves beneath her nightwear. While her blonde hair was currently piled on top of her head he could imagine it sitting in long waves past her shoulders.

He could also imagine her in a really sexy dress and heels.

He said the first thing that came into his head. 'You didn't have anyone else you could stay with?'

It was an innocent enough question. Trouble was, it made her insides curl up a little and made her feel a bit pathetic.

But he wasn't finished. 'Isn't it a bit strange to come and stay with your boss?'

She should have stopped to think for a second. But thinking wasn't really Lara's style—particularly not when she'd just had a glimpse of mind-numbing abs. 'I haven't been in London that long. I originally came from Sheffield so all my friends are up there. And because of the job—looking after Tristan—I haven't really had time to make any good friends since I got here.' She bit the inside of her cheek. 'To be honest, I'm not quite sure what I would have done if Addison had said I couldn't stay.'

She could feel the rush of heat into her cheeks. She felt a bit embarrassed and was definitely squirming. This was rubbish. She wasn't the person who had done anything wrong here. Not like Josh-gets-into-bed-with-the-wrong-woman or Reuben-breaks-into-houses-Tyler. It was time to turn the tables.

'Reuben?'

'Yeah?' He was trying to appear casual as he finished his coffee.

'How, exactly, do you know Caleb?'

She'd stood up to clear the plates away and started loading the dishwasher.

'Why do you want to know?'

'I guess I'm still trying to decide if I'm going to let you stay, or if I'm going to phone the police again.'

He rolled his eyes and gave a casual wave of his hand. 'I knew him years ago.'

She banged the dishwasher closed and pressed a few buttons before sliding back onto the stool across from him. '*Where* did you know him?'

He sighed. 'What's with the interrogation? Isn't it about time to go to bed?' He didn't mean it to come out that way but his voice just naturally inclined upwards as he spoke. It gave the sentence a hint of cheekiness.

Lara's cheeks flushed with colour as she pointedly ignored his comment. 'You asked me how I got the job. It's only fair I ask you how you know Caleb—particularly when I've never seen you around here before.'

Reuben held onto the worktop and leaned back on

the stool. His back was beginning to seize up. He really needed to lie down.

'Caleb and I went to school together.'

'Really? What school?'

He cringed. He knew exactly what came next. 'Eton.'

Her mouth fell open. 'Eton?' He should feel insulted. The surprise wasn't because Caleb had gone to Eton, the surprise was definitely directed at him.

He shrugged his shoulders. 'What can I say? I was a posh boy.'

The colour was starting to die down in her cheeks. It was obvious she was curious. 'It's a long way from Ireland,' she said. It was a natural thing to say but he barely blinked.

'Yes, it is.' It was almost as if he were drawing a line in the sand.

She put her elbows on the worktop and leaned towards him. 'You said you just got back from the US on business. What is it that you do?'

'A bit of this, a bit of that.'

She waggled her finger at him. 'Oh, no. Don't give me that. What is your job title exactly?'

'I'm a businessman.'

She waved her hands. 'And so says the entire population of London.'

'I'm a sports agent.' He said quickly, in the hope it would stop her asking questions.

Her eyes widened. 'You mean you're Jerry Maguire?'

He shook his head. 'If I had a pound for every time I've heard that...'

She perched back up on the stool. 'I like movies but I'm not what you'd call a sports fan. Well, truth be told, I hate sport, but will I know anyone you manage?'

He shrugged. 'If you hate sport, probably not. A few footballers, a few cricketers. One tennis player. Also some basketball and baseball players. A few big-name American footballers.'

She gave him a curious stare. 'So that's why you jet around?'

He paused for a second. 'Most of the time. I have clients in the US, Italy, Spain and England right now. And I'm always looking for the next big signing. Things get a bit crazy at times. It's a mad world out there and sometimes the whole business of a team is based on who they sign—and more importantly how that person behaves. One stupid interview comment can make a team's shares plummet. I sometimes have to do some troubleshooting or some collateral damage limitation. That can take me pretty much anywhere. The US this week, Spain last week. For the next two weeks I'm in London.'

'Lucky me,' she said quickly. He sucked in a breath. For a second he wasn't sure if it had been sarcasm or wit, but then the edges of her mouth turned upwards.

She leaned her head on one of her hands. 'So, if you and Caleb are such lifelong friends, how come you haven't been to see him once in all the time I've worked here?'

He paused to swallow the last of his coffee. 'While it's true that Caleb and I go way back, it's not the same with Addison. Though she's far too polite to come out and say it, I have a strong suspicion that she might not like me very much.'

Lara frowned. Sure, Reuben was annoying, verging on arrogant, but what possible reason did Addison have to actively dislike the man enough to discourage his presence in her home? Should she be worried?

'Why do you think it is exactly that Addison doesn't like you?' She strove to keep her tone neutral and the wobble out of her voice.

He took a few seconds before he answered. 'Let's just say I knew Caleb when we were relatively young guys—

long before Addison came on the scene—and we might have been involved in a few...' he paused to think of the right word '...boisterous activities.'

'Boisterous activities? That's it? That's all you're giving me?'

He nodded. 'I think that would be best.'

She folded her arms across her chest and looked through the kitchen window into the darkness. 'Looks like a long, rainy night out there to me...' She let her voice drift off.

'You've got to be joking? You'd actually ask me to leave?'

She started walking around the kitchen. 'Absolutely. And just think, there's a lovely king-sized bed up there, with fresh, clean sheets just waiting for you to jump in and ease your tired bones.' She folded her arms around herself and rubbed her hands up and down them. She knew exactly how to play him.

He sat down his coffee cup. 'You're a manipulator.'

'And you could be a murderer, a drug dealer or...' she scrunched up her nose '...even worse, a wannabe.'

'A what?' He couldn't hide the surprise in his voice. 'What are you talking about?'

She waved her hand. 'You tell me you're a sports agent, then you tell me you have to sort out badly behaved sports stars. You might just want to hang around them. You might even bring random dubious sport stars back to this place. They could wreck it.'

He shook his head. 'You honestly think I want to hang around these guys? Some of them are worse behaved than two-year-olds.'

She folded her arms across her chest again. 'Then give me a straight answer. Explain your "boisterous activities".'

Boy. She was good. He'd practically walked right into that one.

He stood up, put both hands at his waist and arched

his aching back. 'Fine. We did some cliff-jumping, some free running. There might have been a little police involvement back in the day. Then there was the usual girl stuff. That's probably why Addison doesn't like me. She probably thinks of me as a bad influence or something.'

Lara leaned against one of the white cupboards. 'Why? Because you encouraged her husband to take part in extreme sports, or because of the girl stuff?'

He ran his fingers through his hair. Jet-lag was definitely hitting right now. 'Truth? Probably a bit of both. But, remember, this was all before her time.' It wasn't exactly the truth. But that was as much as he was willing to say.

Lara gave a nod. She'd finished cleaning the kitchen and it was back to its original sparkling white show-home-kitchen appearance. The kind of kitchen that looked as if people didn't actually live in the house. 'Well, that's okay, then.'

She was still watching him with those wary blue eyes. He was trying not to think about the idiot who'd cheated on her and was obviously short of a few brain cells.

'I've got an idea,' he said, as he walked back through to the sitting room and picked up her half-empty bottle of wine and glass. 'Let's have a toast.'

'A toast to what?' She looked completely bewildered.

'A toast to the fact we'll need to share this house for the next two weeks.'

He poured some wine into her glass and handed it to her before she could object, then lifted the bottle up towards her. 'To an interesting two weeks.' He clinked the bottle to her glass before lifting it to his lips.

Her eyes never left his. 'To an interesting two weeks,' she repeated.

CHAPTER THREE

It was the weirdest feeling. Somewhere in the space up above her there was another body breathing in and out.

She'd bet Reuben wasn't having trouble sleeping. At first she'd thought she was too hot and had discarded the thick onesie. After tonight she'd probably never wear it again. Then she'd realised she didn't have PJs—and sleeping in the nude with a stranger in the house just wasn't an option. So she'd done something she'd never even thought about before and crept along the corridor to Addison and Caleb's room and rummaged through a few drawers until she'd found something suitable.

But it wasn't entirely suitable. Addison's sleeping apparel seemed to be short satin nighties—a whole variety of them. Even lying in bed she kept trying to tug it over her backside as it left her feeling strangely exposed. Or maybe that was just because Reuben was overhead.

She couldn't help it. She'd done an online search on him. Who wouldn't?

He seemed to be the darling of the acidic football critics. He'd brought two young, unknown Argentinian footballers to a Premiership team and had virtually saved it from bankruptcy. He'd negotiated a change of coach three times for his tennis player, which had helped him shoot up the rankings. He'd had seven baseball teams fighting over one of his players. And the dollar signs for his latest basketball signing made her eyes water.

Then there were the photos. Plenty with the latest sports

star but she was more interested in the ones with a beauty by his side. Granted, the beauty was never the same twice. But all were considerably more glamorous than she was— even when she was wearing one of Addison's satin night-dresses.

Eventually she heard noise downstairs. Had she slept at all? It didn't feel like it. It felt as if she'd tossed and turned all night, her head full of dark-clothed strangers breaking into the house.

By the sound of it Reuben was banging through all the cupboards in the kitchen. Lara sighed and threw back the bedclothes. She sat up, the cooler morning hair hitting her barely covered skin. She glanced around. She wasn't going to go downstairs dressed like this. She hesitated in the doorway, peering along the corridor before stealing down the corridor to Addison and Caleb's bedroom again in search of a dressing gown.

She should have guessed. There was a perfect matching bright pink satin dressing gown to the nightdress she was wearing. Bright pink trimmed with purple lace. She didn't even want to think what it had actually cost. She wrapped the dressing gown around her. That was much better. It covered all the parts of her it should, skimming just above her knees.

With a bit more confidence she opened the door to head towards the kitchen and almost barrelled straight into tea-bearing Reuben.

'Oops, sorry.'

She jumped back as the tea sloshed onto the carpet.

Caleb's eyes swept up and down her more exposed body. 'Nice change,' he said quickly. 'So you don't al-ways dress as a teddy bear.' He squinted behind her. 'Is that Caleb's room?'

Heat flushed into her cheeks. How did this guy do that

to her? She bit her lip. 'Caught. Just don't tell. Let's just say I didn't bring a lot of nightwear with me.'

He looked as if he were going to say something but stopped and gave his head a shake. He held the tea out towards her. 'I made you tea.'

She stared at the cup. 'What are you up to?'

He gave her a smile. 'What makes you think I'm up to something?'

'It's written all over your face.'

He sighed. 'What are your plans for today?'

Her eyes dipped downwards to her pink-painted toes. She hadn't realised it but they actually matched her night-dress and gown. Her toes curled. 'I'm not actually sure.'

'You would have been on holiday, right? What were you going to do?'

She bit the inside of her cheek and said nothing.

This time it was Reuben's turn to blush as he realised her obvious change of plans. 'Oh, right. You were plan-ning on spending time with that numbnut that you called a boyfriend. That means you're free for the next two weeks.'

Her head shot up. 'What did you call him?'

Reuben shrugged. 'A numbnut—which he obviously is. Does the guy think he's some kind of superhero? How dare he cheat on you?' His eyes narrowed. 'Want to get thinking creatively? We could plot some hideous revenge.'

Her hands closed around the cup of tea. 'Revenge means thinking about him—I'd rather not.'

Reuben nodded. 'I have some work to do. Do you fancy coming with me?' What was wrong with him? He had a mountain of work to get through. He knew there were six hundred emails in his inbox. But he had some other things to do. And he was feeling sorry for her. This time his eyes lingered on her curves and long bare legs.

'I suppose I'd better register somewhere to try and find a new rental in London.'

'Do you have the name of a reputable agency?'

She nodded. 'The one I used the last time was great. I guess I'll just register with them again.' She sighed. 'Once I've done that, I think I need to do a little shopping.'

'Food or clothes?' He'd already checked out the kitchen. After last night's feast there was hardly anything left.

She sighed again. 'Both, I suppose.'

'Well, come and hang out with me for a while, then we can do some shopping.'

She looked at him suspiciously.

He lifted his hands. 'What? It's only fair I foot the bill for shopping. I ate all your food last night.'

She nodded. 'Okay, then. Let me drink this tea and find some clothes.'

He gave a cheery nod and wandered back down the corridor. She watched his retreating back, but her eyes were drawn downwards. He was still wearing well-fitting jeans and a snug grey T-shirt.

Her two weeks of misery seemed to be looking up.

CHAPTER FOUR

HE MUST BE CRAZY. Why on earth had he invited Lara out for the day?

Sure, she was cute. Sure, they had to share a house for the next two weeks. But that didn't mean he had to try and be her new best friend.

But there had been something about her. When she'd been telling him about her ex and the pain had been etched in her eyes. The guy was clearly a fool.

He'd cringed last night when she'd asked him why Addison didn't like him. He tried his best not to think about that night at all. But Lara had seemed placated when he'd padded out his story with a little detail.

Too bad he'd left the biggest detail out.

Caleb had shrugged off what had happened between them. He knew how damaged Reuben had been by his parents' relationship. But Addison had no idea. He still wasn't Mr Popular with her.

She probably didn't even know that Caleb had invited him to stay here.

He finished sending a few emails as Lara walked into the kitchen. She was wearing a pink sequined T-shirt, a pair of hip-hugging blue jeans, black heeled boots and a fitted bright pink raincoat.

Her hair was soft and shiny and hanging in waves around her shoulders. She walked across the kitchen, smiling, pulled a pink lipstick from her pocket and painted it on her lips. 'Reuben, what exactly did you plan today? I should remind you, I'm not exactly a sports fan.'

He laughed. 'It will be fine, I promise. I need to visit one of the nearby football stadiums but I'll be less than half an hour. Then we can sort out some food and anything else you need to buy.'

She gave a thoughtful nod. 'I might have left some of my things behind.'

'Things like what?'

She sighed. 'My whole summer wardrobe. Just about everything I need to put in my case for my holiday is still at the flat. It's ready to be picked up. It's all sitting in another case.'

He blinked. 'No problem. We'll swing by later and you can collect it.'

Panic streaked across her face. 'But...I don't think... I'm not sure...'

'Calm down.' He reached over and took her hand, trying to ignore the little pulses he could feel in his palm, '*I'll* go and get your things.'

Her eyes widened, flooding with relief. 'You will?'

How on earth could he say no? 'Of course I will. No problem.'

He picked up his car keys. 'Now, can we go?'

For some strange reason the car seemed to be parting the traffic in London. Lara had never managed to get through the London streets so quickly—but, then again, she'd never been in a car like this one before either. The dark red colour alone seemed to command attention but it was so low, so sleek against the road that she wondered if she'd ever be able to get out again.

Reuben handled the car with ease. In the streets of London she would be terrified to drive a hundred yards but he took every corner without a second thought, pulling up outside the vast stadium only thirty minutes later.

He signalled to her to get out and she climbed out, looking up at the glass-fronted stadium. 'Come on, I won't be long,' he said, as he walked into the reception area, waving at the reception staff. 'Lydia, Carrie, where's the chairman?'

'Downstairs in the changing rooms. He's talking to the manager.'

Reuben gave a casual wave and opened a door to a flight of stairs. Lara struggled to keep up with his long strides, almost running to keep up as he turned corner after corner through a warren of tunnels underneath the club.

He paused outside one of the doors. 'Wait here,' he said, smiling. 'Don't want you to see anything you shouldn't.' He disappeared through the door.

She sighed and leaned against the concrete wall. This wasn't exactly her idea of fun. How long would this take?

A few seconds later there were shouts and one of the footballers came stomping along the corridor. His eyes only briefly brushed over her before he pulled his top over his head and banged through the changing-room door.

She sucked in a deep breath. Footballers were known for being temperamental, weren't they?

A few seconds later the door opened and another footballer came out. This time he had a hint of smile about his face. Which was just as well, since he wasn't wearing much. Lara sucked in an even deeper breath than before and fixed her eyes on her hands. This guy slammed through another door with 'Physio' emblazoned across it.

Then came another, then another, each man wearing a little less than the one before.

Did the players always walk around here practically naked? She had about a hundred friends who would think this a fabulous dream. Pity she wasn't one of them.

Lara focused on her fingernails. They weren't great. When was the last time she'd taken time out for a mani- cure? It had been on her to-do list. It would need to move further up. There was another bang. She couldn't possi- bly ignore it.

Her chin bounced off the floor. It was the team's star mega-million-pound footballer, with painted-on sculpted abs, a pair of teeny-weeny white tight briefs and the best spray tan she'd ever seen. His eyes looked her up and down lasciviously, making her stomach roll over—and not in a good way. His ego was so big there was barely room for the rest of him.

'Hey, baby,' he said, as he slid along the corridor to- wards her.

She gulped. Oh, no. Her worst nightmare. She was *so* out of her depth right now.

The door opened behind her and an arm slid around her shoulder. 'Chris, are you being a prat again?' He turned towards her. 'Sorry, Lara, I should have warned you about these guys. If there are any females around they like to do walk-bys with each one wearing less than the previous one. Ignore them.' Reuben had a wet towel in his hand and he flicked it at Chris, who leapt into the air like a big girl.

'Ouch!' He rubbed his thigh and stormed back into the changing room, muttering expletives under his breath.

Lara shook her head. 'You're joking—that's what they do?'

Reuben nodded. 'Every time. They can't help it. The average mental age around here is about twelve.'

He hadn't moved his arm from her shoulders and she wasn't quite sure how she felt about it. Exactly how many women did he bring here with him—and why did that matter to her? 'Can we get out of here now?'

He smiled. A white straight-toothed smile that reached all the way to those big brown eyes she was currently staring up into. It was odd. But it was one of the most genuine smiles she'd seen. Before, he'd been amused by her or he'd been sarcastic. This time it felt real and it sent a little wave of pulses skittering over her skin. Just what she needed while her brain was mush.

She gave a little shudder and put her head down as they walked down the corridor. But Reuben stopped. 'Hey, what is it?'

Her footsteps had stopped but she hadn't lifted her head. He stepped in front of her, his fingers reaching down and tilting her chin up towards him.

It seemed such a personal touch—an almost intimate touch. Or as intimate as you could be in a place filled with staff while you were fully clothed. 'What's wrong, Lara?'

It was the way he said her name. That Irish lilt that was guaranteed to turn any woman's legs to jelly. This guy could be Colin Farrell's brother.

Her body wanted to tremble. But she wouldn't let it. No way. No, sir.

She lifted her eyes to meet his. 'Let's just say I have an image from yesterday imprinted permanently on my brain. It keeps flashing back in there when it's least wanted.'

He gave a visible shudder. She didn't need to give an explicit description. He knew exactly what she was getting at.

He swung his arm back around her shoulders. 'It's time to move things on. Let's go and collect the stuff you need for your summer holidays and that way you're done—finished. For ever. You can forget about the loser and look forward to your holiday.'

He guided her back along the corridor. 'I meant to ask—where are you going on holiday anyway?'

He pushed the door open and held it for her. 'I'm booked to go on a cruise,' she sighed. 'I always wanted to cruise around the Med so I saved all my spare pennies for it.' She waved her hand. 'And if you're going to cruise, you need the clothes for it.'

He smiled as if an idea had just blossomed in his brain. 'You certainly do. Where does the ship sail to?'

She was starting to feel a little more comfortable around Reuben. Talking about travelling meant that they were on neutral ground. Small talk was about all she could handle right now. She smiled. 'Everywhere I've always wanted to visit—Barcelona, Monte Carlo, Pisa, Marseille, Sicily.' A little edge came to her voice. 'I'm not going to let him spoil it for me.'

Reuben nodded. 'And we won't. Let's get this over and done with.'

If someone had sat him down before he'd boarded the flight to London and told him what his next twenty-four hours would be like he wouldn't have believed them. Not for a second.

He rapped the door of the Camden flat once again, glancing down to the street to where his car was idling. Even from here he could see Lara's hands turning over and over in her lap.

There was a noise—a grunt—and the door finally opened.

Reuben blinked. Really? Lara was definitely hovering around a ten. This guy? He was lucky if he was a four. What's more, he could almost smell the arrogance coming from him. His fingers automatically balled into fists.

'Who are you?' said Mr Barely Dressed. That paunch really wasn't attractive. There was a tittering noise behind him. Great. The neighbour was still hanging around.

'I'm a friend of Lara's. I'm here to pick up the rest of her stuff.'

The guy's brow furrowed. 'A friend of Lara's? I've never met you before.'

'And you'll never meet me again. Now, she wants her case with her summer clothes in it. Give it to me and we'll be on our way.'

Now the guy looked really pleased with himself. 'Well, it's too late. I flung the rest of her stuff out of the flat yesterday after she stormed out. The bin men have already been.' He folded his arms across his chest.

'You what?' He couldn't stop himself. He had Mr Smarmy pinned against the wall in an instant. 'You did what?'

The guy panicked. 'Well, she was gone. And it's not like she'll be coming back. Why would I want to keep her stuff?'

Reuben shook his head. 'It's not bad enough you got caught in bed with another woman, you didn't even give Lara the chance to collect all her things. How dare you?'

The guy was still against the wall but he lifted his hands, doing his best impression of a shrug. 'Well, she was screaming and shouting yesterday. Calling me all kinds of names. There was no way she'd be back.'

A woman appeared at his elbow, holding a phone in her hand. 'If you don't get out of here now I'm calling the police.' She turned her nose up in a sneer. 'Tell Lara she's not welcome here.'

There was so much he could say. His temper was bubbling just beneath the surface. What a pair of low-lives. The woman was running her eyes up and down his body. It made him feel positively unclean. Both of them did.

He could feel adrenaline surging within him, closely followed by a red mist descending. Just like he had the night he'd punched out Caleb. Was it any wonder Addison didn't like him? He flinched. He didn't want to be that guy any more. He was *trying* not to be that guy any more.

He released his grip on the guy and looked at him in

disgust. 'You two deserve each other. Lara's worth ten of you.'

He turned on his heel, ignoring the shouts that followed him. The guy made him mad. The girl made him mad. Their utter disrespect of Lara made him mad. How had she ended mixed up with these two?

He strode back to the car, jumped inside and slammed the door, not thinking for a second about what he was going to say to her.

Her eyes widened at the expression on his face and she stared at his empty hands. 'Didn't you get my stuff?'

It was the wide-eyed innocence that made his stomach curl in knots. On a few fleeting moments Lara had appeared quite street savvy, but right now? He felt as if he were just about to grab her heart between both hands and squeeze hard.

She'd already told him she'd saved hard for her dream holiday—and from what he'd seen he could take a guess that the guy upstairs hadn't contributed at all. Just how much would it cost her to replace her entire summer holiday wardrobe?

'I'm picking your stuff up later,' he said quickly.

He turned the car onto the main road. 'Now, let's go and food shop.'

She wasn't quite sure when the house burglar turned into her kind of guardian angel. All she knew was thirty minutes after telling her they'd pick up her clothes later he pulled his sleek car up outside one of the most famous department stores in London with its gold and green sign.

Reuben walked around and opened the door for her. Her head flicked from side to side. 'You can't leave your car here...'

Her voice trailed off as a uniformed man slid into the driver's seat and the car mysteriously disappeared.

He smiled at the expression on her face and gestured towards the door. 'Let's hit the food court. We need to buy supplies.'

She watched the dark red car disappear around the corner, shaking her head as he slung his arm back around her shoulders and steered her towards the entrance. 'I didn't even know they did that,' she murmured.

'What can I say? I've friends in high places.'

What on earth did that mean? She looked down at her clothes. Jeans and a pink t-shirt. And come to think of it her boots could do with a polish. If she'd known they were shopping in style she might have dressed up a little.

They walked down the stairs to the food court. Even two steps down the aroma of everything expensive came up to meet them.

Reuben was smiling already, crossing over to the glass display cabinet of fine meats and truffles and *foie gras*.

'What do you like?' he asked.

She wrinkled her nose. 'Chicken.'

He raised his eyebrows. 'Chicken?' You'd think she'd sworn out loud.

She nodded. 'Chicken. I like chicken.'

She looked around at the massive department.

'And raspberry jam. And freshly baked bread—maybe a croissant or two. And some more bacon and eggs.'

Her legs had started walking, following her nose as she glanced from side to side.

'I love the chocolate digestives from here, and the rose and violet shortbread— Oh...' She spun round and put her hand on his chest. 'And those tiny dark chocolates filled with orange. Now, where on earth will they be?'

He put one hand on his hip as people filed past. 'We're in one of the finest food stores and you want bacon. And eggs. And raspberry jam.' His chest was right in front of her nose and now every time she breathed in she didn't get the wonderful food aromas around her, she just got Reuben Tyler. Every masculine, woody scent of him. If she could sell that aftershave she'd never have to work again.

She breathed in, trying not to look like a teenager. Her hand was still resting on his chest. Through his thin T-shirt she could feel the warmth of his skin and the roughened hairs underneath the palm of her hand. Her brain tried to make sense of things.

This time yesterday she hadn't known this man. She hadn't even known he existed.

'Chicken.' The word came out of nowhere. 'You forgot the chicken.'

She tilted her head and smiled up at him. Her nose was directly across from his chest. Too close for comfort really. Especially now she could see the tiny shadow along his jaw line. Why did her hand want to reach up and touch it?

His arm folded around her waist and he pulled her closer and spun her around as a large group of tourists swept past. He was looking down at her with those deep brown eyes. It was almost as if he knew she was a little mesmerised. Truth was, he must be used to it.

'Didn't want you to get trampled.' He laughed as his accent played havoc with her senses. 'And chicken.' He shook his head again. 'Let's not forget the chicken.'

He reached behind her, his chin brushing against her hair, and plucked a thin cylindrical box from a stand. 'Your orange creams, I suppose?'

She closed her hands around the tube. 'Perfect.'

He paused. It was almost as if something else flitted past his brain. He was leaning over her, seeing every part of her up close and personal. If he tilted his chin down just a touch...

She wished she'd put on more make-up—heavier foundation instead of her usual tinted moisturiser. Longer-lasting lipstick rather than her light lip tint.

She could almost feel herself disintegrate under his gaze. What did he see? And how did she compare to what he was used to?

She tried to squeeze that thought from her mind. Why should she care? She barely knew him. So what if he'd just gone out of his way to help her? The truth was he was still invading the space she'd thought she would have for the next two weeks. Her skin was prickling under his intense gaze. There was a whole wave of sensations sweeping across her. And she couldn't fathom any one of them.

Reuben gave a little shake and stepped back. It was almost as if nothing had happened. He pulled up a trolley next to them and started loading up his selection from the counter. He pointed to item after item and she blinked at the price tags. Chicken stuffed with haggis and wrapped in bacon. Chicken with chorizo and a tomato sauce. Chicken with peppered sauce and mushrooms all packaged up before her eyes. If she hadn't been hungry before she was definitely hungry now.

And it seemed once Reuben started to shop he could do it like a pro. Sirloin steaks—enough to last the fortnight. More pepper sauce. Salad. Fresh bread, pastries and croissants. Her raspberry jam. Bacon, eggs and sausages. A whole heap of vegetables. Biscuits, chocolates and a really, really good-looking fresh cream gateau.

Lara looked at the groaning trolley and nudged him.

'What?' he asked.

'I don't think people really do their weekly shop in here,' she whispered, her eyes taking in the other customers, who had maybe one or two items in their hands. 'At this rate we'll need to remortgage Caleb's house for the food bill.'

He looked surprised. 'I'm covering the food bill. Don't worry. You didn't expect me there and I should contribute something.'

He made it all sound so reasonable, while her purse was currently screaming out in relief. There was no way she could pay half of a bill like this. 'Fancy a bottle of wine?' he asked, as they walked further along.

She glanced at the nearest shelf. Two hundred pounds a bottle. 'Er...no, thanks.'

He moved the trolley forward then stopped again. 'It was rosé you were drinking last night, wasn't it?'

He put three bottles in the trolley before she had a chance to answer, then he picked a bottle of red and one of white too. She could feel herself breaking out in a cold sweat at these prices. It didn't matter that she wasn't footing the bill.

She leaned forward and hissed in his ear, 'Put those back. You can buy wine for less than ten pounds a bottle in the supermarket down the road.'

The corners of his lips turned up in amusement. He walked over to the nearest cash register and handed over his credit card without anything being run up. The cashier nodded, swiped it and handed it back, taking a note of the ticket for his car.

He slipped an arm around her back and led her to the stairs. Lara's head was turned backwards, staring at the cashier. 'Really? You don't even put in your PIN?'

He shook his head. 'I trust these people. By the time we want to leave the car will be loaded up and ready to go.'

She shook her head as she climbed the stairs. The jewellery section was right in front of them. 'Let's go upstairs for a coffee. Food shopping makes me hungry.' Now, *that* she could agree with.

She wandered through the jewellery department—most of the jewellery didn't have price tags, which told her everything she needed to know. While she didn't know how much things actually cost, she could just do her little-girl-in-a-shop state of mind and pretend that they could all be hers.

She stopped suddenly and Reuben walked right into her. She hadn't realised he was so close. 'Sorry,' she murmured.

He followed her eyeline to the side and pointed. 'You're looking at that?' His face was screwed up in that a-guy-will-never-understand kind of way.

She nodded. 'It's gorgeous. It's like something Cleopatra would wear.' She moved a little closer but resisted the temptation to touch the glass. Interlocked flat panels of white, yellow and rose gold. One of the fashion magazines would probably describe it as a showstopper. And it was.

She moved further along and stopped and pointed at a large square-cut pink diamond surrounded by white diamonds. She was too scared to even breathe next to it. 'Bet we'd really need to remortgage Caleb's house for that.'

Reuben shook his head and steered her towards the lift. The smell of coffee hit them as soon as the lift doors opened, in perfect timing with a loud growl from Reuben's stomach.

She laughed. 'Trying to tell me something?'

He nodded. 'My body is telling you that it's crying out for another bacon sandwich.' He pointed to the glass-fronted cabinet filled with tiny cakes. 'But that's not what you get here.'

She turned to face him. 'Did you want to go somewhere else?' She got the distinct impression he'd brought her here because he'd thought she'd prefer it. On most days she would be happy with a cup of tea in a local café. Why did she get the impression he was trying to keep on her good side?

He shook his head. 'The coffee is great in here. Makes up for the lack of bacon. What are you having?'

She stared at the board as the barista approached them. 'I'll have a skinny, sugar-free caramel latte,' she said.

'What?' He wrinkled his nose as the barista waved her hand.

'I've got it,' she said, as she turned to the large metal machine. 'Triple shot for you, Reuben?'

He nodded then turned back to Lara. 'Didn't take you for one of those mumbo-jumbo crazy coffee girls. Not after the amount of chocolate you consumed last night.'

She slapped his arm. 'Hey. Anyway, there's method in my madness. The skinny sugar-free counteracts the fact I'm going to have four of those little cakes.' She was feeling quite pleased with herself. The only problem would be choosing. She walked up and down the counter, trying to decide.

'Only four?' came the deep voice, right next to her ear.

She jumped. 'Stop it.' And turned back to the counter. The barista had finished preparing the coffees and placed them on a tray. She must be able to read minds because she was standing with an empty plate and a pair of tongs in her hand.

'A rhubarb and custard tart, a death by chocolate, a strawberry and vanilla pastry and a pecan pie.' The words were out before she could stop them and Reuben let out a muffled laugh behind her.

He pointed in the other direction. 'I'll have a piece of apple pie,' he said, before leaning over towards her ear again. 'Man-sized.'

Her head shot around and she felt heat sear into her cheeks. It was ridiculous. He was only winding her up. There was even a dangerous twinkle in his eyes.

She went into her bag to find her purse but he waved her away. 'You just bought the shopping. You've got to let me pay for something.'

'We'll talk about it later.' She sighed and made her

way over to a table, pulling out one of comfortable velvet chairs and sitting down.

Reuben sat down opposite her and put the tray of coffee and plates on the tables.

She pointed at his apple pie, which was obliterated from view with cream. 'Would you like some apple pie to go with your cream?'

He picked up his fork and speared the pie. 'You can talk. At least I've only got one instead of four.'

She picked up her tiny pecan pie. 'It's ridiculous calling this thing a pie. Look, it's barely bigger than my thumbnail. One bite and it'll be gone. Two if I nibble.' She eyed his plate again and couldn't hide her smile. 'You, on the other hand, could sink to the bottom of the Thames eating that lot.'

He shook his head and kept eating. There was something nice about this. Something easy. After yesterday morning she'd thought the next month would be an absolute disaster. She could write a book on the last twenty-four hours alone.

But being around Reuben Tyler wasn't as hard or as uncomfortable as she'd first thought. It didn't hurt that he was particularly easy on the eye. And that accent...

She watched him carefully from across the table. She could see a few women giving him a second glance then giving *her* a second glance too.

He may not be a footballer but he looked like the kind of guy who'd have a WAG hanging around him and there was no way she fitted the bill.

'So what did you plan to do for the next two weeks?' He'd finished demolishing his pie.

She shrugged her shoulders. 'I was just going to hang out with Josh, preparing for our holiday.' She wrinkled her face. 'I guess that won't be happening.'

Reuben's dark eyes were fixed on her. 'Do you want that to happen?'

'What? No, of course not. Not after what I saw yesterday.' She shuddered. 'It's going to take a long time to get that sight out of my mind.'

He was still watching. 'You sounded as if you were a bit sorry.'

She took a sip of her latte. 'About Josh?' It was hard to find the words. 'Part of me is, and part of me isn't.' She picked up her spoon and started stirring her latte. It was an unconscious act, keeping her eyes away from his penetrating gaze. 'I guess I've been looking forward to the holiday for so long that I just pushed the other stuff away.'

'What other stuff?'

Her insides started to squirm. It was bad enough having to think these thoughts to herself. They'd definitely come to fruition last night. But saying them out loud? That was something else entirely.

She kept stirring as the swirling coffee was easy to focus on. 'Probably the fact that Josh hadn't paid for any of the holiday. Hadn't paid rent since we moved in together after we got back from Oz, and didn't seem particularly bothered about finding a job. He was just happy that I was working and paying the bills.'

Her fingers clenched around the long spoon. 'Now I just think what an idiot I was. Out working while he was at home, doing goodness knows what.'

His hand reached across the table and covered hers. 'Don't put yourself down, Lara. You're a gorgeous girl who just got stuck with a loser. Lesson learned. Move on.'

She gulped. All of a sudden her mouth was dry and the rhubarb and custard tart had just stuck midway down her throat. It was his hand. The way it just enveloped hers. The warmth. That little touch of compassion.

After the rubbish day she'd had yesterday, she hadn't

really expected anyone to reach out to her. To make her feel valued again.

It gave her a warm feeling. The kind that had always spread over her when she used to be around her gran. Her parents had been great, but she'd always had a special connection with her gran. She'd encouraged her studies in English and had been so proud of her when she'd been accepted at university. But when her gran had died one month later it had all been too much for her. Her mum and dad loved her lots—but had never had the same ambitions for her that her gran had. She'd needed some time away—some space. She'd deferred her university placement and drifted from one bad job and bad relationship to the next, finally ending up in Australia then back here.

Tears were brimming in her eyes. Thank goodness Reuben hadn't noticed. Was he getting a tiny pulse shooting up his arm too?

He gave her hand another squeeze and went back to his coffee. Obviously not.

She was an idiot.

It was almost as if he could read part of her mind. See that she was trying to hide the parts of her that were hurt. His tongue ran along his lips, catching some of the sugar from the apple tart, and she swallowed, trying not to stare.

'Caleb's been good for me.' It was as if he chose the words carefully.

She was curious. 'How?'

He pressed his lips together. 'He keeps me focused. Keeps me grounded. Addison might not like me much, but when I go to their house and see Caleb with his son...' His voice tailed off and he gave a little shrug, 'It makes me see what a family should be like. I don't doubt for a second Caleb would give his life for his wife or his son in a heartbeat. They're his whole world.'

There was something about the way he said the words

that sent a little prickle down her spine. She didn't doubt for a second her mum and dad would do the same thing for her. Reuben hadn't mentioned his family at all. 'Aren't all families like that?' she asked carefully.

His gaze caught hers for a second and he shook his head. 'That's one of the things I like about you, Lara—your idealism.' He took another swig of his coffee. 'So what are your plans now for the rest of this week?'

It was clear that part of the conversation was over. She couldn't pry—she barely knew him—so she swallowed the remainder of her tart and said the first thing that came into her head. 'I've decided to do some touristy stuff. I never really got the chance when I first moved to London, so it might be quite nice.'

He looked amused. He tilted his head to the side. 'What kind of thing?'

'I'm going to do the Buckingham Palace tour.' Where had that come from? It was the first thing that had popped into her head and right now she didn't want to look like an idiot in front of Reuben. She certainly didn't want to act like a woman who'd been cheated on and mope about the place. This was the new improved version of herself.

A woman swept by their table in red-soled black patent stiletto heels and a long sweeping cream wool coat. Her long blonde hair was like a sheen from a TV advert and Lara sensed the cool blonde's eyes sweeping over her and then Reuben.

'Reuben Tyler?'

Perfect pouting pink lips appeared at the table, along with a waft of expensive perfume and a remortgage-your-house handbag. Lara shrank back in her chair.

Reuben froze for a few milliseconds then seemed to move into his default charm position. 'Millicent. How nice to see you.' He stood up for a second and let her do the kiss-on-both-cheeks move.

'When did you get back?' Millicent's voice was a little sharp.

'Last night.'

'Really? I didn't notice your car.' Lara could feel the edges of her mouth start to turn upwards. Watching the body language here was a real treat. For a few seconds she'd felt intimidated by the gorgeous statuesque blonde. But while Reuben had his charm face in place it was clear the woman was about as welcome as a box of frogs.

She lifted her latte for a sip and prepared to attack her death by chocolate. Better settle in. This could be fun.

Reuben shook his head. 'There's work being done of the roof. Asbestos. So I can't stay there right now.'

Millicent tilted her head to the side, the tone of her voice changing automatically. 'Why didn't you say? You're more than welcome to come and bunk in with me.' She let out a shrill little laugh.

'I hardly think that would be appropriate,' said Reuben. 'Millicent, meet Lara, my girlfriend.'

The perfectly formed death by chocolate cake somersaulted out of her hand and landed upside down on the white and black tiled floor. She stared in disbelief at her little piece of heaven before shooting Reuben a laser glare.

Millicent was practically sneering as her eyes swept over Lara's less-than-perfect hairstyle, minimal make-up and non-designer clothes.

Her recovery was swift. 'Oh, how nice. Reuben...' she glared at him '...was obviously keeping you a secret.'

She extended her expertly manicured hand towards Lara. Lara stared at her chocolate-smudged fingers and wiped them on a napkin, reaching over and shaking Millicent's hand. 'You too.'

'Where do you live?' asked Millicent quickly.

A thousand tempting answers flooded through her brain. Part of her wanted to give the world's most exclusive address—to say *Buckingham Palace*—and the other part of her wanted to pretend to live in the most notorious part of London, just to see how Millicent would react.

She put on her best face as she nudged Reuben under the table with her boot. To his credit he didn't even flinch.

'Belgravia,' she said. It wasn't exactly a lie. She *was* living there—for the next two weeks at least.

'Oh...' Millicent gave an almost disbelieving nod of her head. 'How lovely.'

'Well, it was lovely to see you again, Millicent,' Reuben said quickly. He might as well have put a sign above their heads saying, *Go away. Now.*

Instead, he did something much more unexpected. He leaned across the table and grabbed hold of the lapel of Lara's jacket. It pulled her forward just a few inches and that was enough for Reuben to lock his lips onto hers.

For a second she couldn't breathe. He'd stood up and leaned all the way across the table. She could taste coffee. She could taste apple. But what she didn't get—not for a second—was how good his lips felt against hers.

This was no tender kiss. No tiny peck. His other hand reached across and fastened at the back of her head, almost holding her in position. She could have objected. She should have objected. But something else was happening. Her lips were starting to move against his. For some unknown reason her body was starting to waken and fire on all cylinders. He didn't need his hand at the back of her head. She couldn't have pulled away even if she'd wanted to.

The kiss deepened, his lips opened against hers, his tongue nudging along the edges of her lips. It was only natural to let her own lips open to his. Her brain was in a swirl. What on earth was she doing?

Then, almost as soon as it had begun, it was over. Reuben pulled away, sitting back with a cheeky gleam in his eyes and leaving her stunned.

After a few seconds she almost remembered to breathe.

Millicent gave an almost discernible sniff then swept away in her stilettos as if she had been born to wear them—and she probably had been. Lara watched in slight awe. If that had been her she would be sprawled on her back by now.

She turned her steely gaze to Reuben and arched her brows. She couldn't have formed words if she'd tried.

He actually shifted a little in his seat. Apart from when she'd bashed him over the head this was the first time he'd actually looked a little uncomfortable. Good.

He gave a little gulp. 'I think I might have just crossed the line there.'

'You're so far over the line, you can't even see it any more. It's just a speck on the landscape. Is that how you roll? You just grab unsuspecting women for a kiss?'

He had the decency to look a little sheepish. He pointed towards the food. 'I try to soften the blow first with coffee and cake.'

She stared hard at him. Her mind was still tumbling over and over *that kiss*. The kiss that had made her heart race erratically, her mind go numb and woken up parts of her she'd thought were dead. Kisses weren't meant to do that. Or certainly not a kiss with no preamble, no flirting, and in a public place.

'I know. I'm sorry.' He leaned across the table towards her. 'Desperate times call for desperate measures. Want to know what my friends and I actually call Millicent?'

Her curiosity spiked immediately. She just hoped it wasn't some crude boy thing. She was trying not to focus on the logical part of her brain that had recognised he'd just said he'd had to be desperate to kiss her. 'Okay,' she said cautiously.

He glanced around, almost as if he expected Millicent to spring out again from behind the nearest pillar. 'The barracuda.'

Lara choked. 'What?'

He nodded. 'Honestly. She's a nightmare. So I'm sorry about the girlfriend thing and the kiss thing, but it was the quickest way to get rid of her without being rude.'

'So ignoring her and kissing me wasn't rude, then?'

Reuben's eyes twinkled as he leaned back in his chair. 'You can't say it was all bad, was it?'

She ignored the cheeky comment. The guy was a player. And she was feeling a little wicked. It seemed like kissing a bad boy brought out the worst in her.

Lara fiddled with her last tiny cake—the strawberry and vanilla pastry. 'I have a price, you know,' she said carefully.

Reuben sat back. He looked a tiny bit worried. 'What do you mean?'

She pointed behind him to the glass cabinet. 'It will take at least another four deaths by chocolate since you killed my last one.'

He breathed a sigh of relief and grinned. 'Absolutely.' He stood up and walked back over to the counter, coming back moments later with a pile of tiny chocolate cakes all topped with cream. He pushed them across the table towards her. 'Go on. Do your worst.'

She pulled the plate towards her and picked up a fork. 'If you keep feeding me like this I won't be able to fit into my bikinis and summer dresses.'

Something flickered across his face. She'd no idea what. He looked as if he'd just swallowed something unpleasant but he recovered quickly.

She wasn't entirely sure what she thought of Reuben Tyler, but it might be fun finding out.

* * *

His insides coiled up. He was going to have to tell her soon. Lara wasn't a designer shopper, but any woman's high street summer wardrobe would still cost a lot to replace. He got the distinct impression that while she managed, Lara wasn't exactly flush with money and given that she'd now have to scrape together the deposit to rent a new flat, the last thing he wanted to do was let her know she needed to buy a whole new summer wardrobe.

'I've been thinking about the cruise,' she said, gazing across the café. 'I think I'll need to get a few more things. A new pair of sandals and maybe another skirt. But I won't know for sure until I can go through the rest of my summer clothes.'

Reuben shifted uncomfortably in his chair. It was now or never. He really needed to be honest with her. He licked his dry lips. 'About your summer clothes...' he started.

'What?' All of a sudden her voice and eyes were razor sharp. He could almost feel her gaze penetrate his skin. What was it with women and their senses? They could practically smell when something was wrong.

For the first time in his life words stuck in his throat. What was wrong with him? He'd never been a stranger to the truth—in fact, he'd often been criticised for his direct approach.

'Maybe you should get some new things,' he said slowly, trying to pick his words carefully. 'Cruises are quite glamorous, aren't they?'

'You don't think I'm glamorous enough?' The words shot out and he cringed.

'No. No, that's not what I meant at all.'

'Then what did you mean?' Women didn't usually make him squirm. This was a first for Reuben Tyler.

Her gaze was fixed on him. Like some kind of female superhero with laser vision. Who could have guessed the girl that had been the giant pink teddy bear could do a complete turnaround?

She was doing her best to appear direct. To have a little edge. Trouble was, he already knew her a little better than that. He'd seen the vulnerability in her eyes. He'd seen the hurt. And he didn't want to be the person responsible for that.

He leaned his elbow on the table and rested his head on his hand. 'There might have been a bit of an issue with Josh.'

Her eyes narrowed. 'What kind of issue?'

'He might have disposed of the rest of your clothes.'

'He *what*?'

Heads all over shot round. A few of the counter staff stood up on their toes, trying to see who'd yelled, but since Lara was on her feet it was pretty obvious.

Reuben could feel all the gazes turn to him. Yeah, right. This was all his fault.

He gave the slightest shrug. 'Sorry. The guy's obviously an idiot. He said he'd dumped all your stuff when I asked.'

She leaned across the table towards him. 'And you knew this? You knew this a few hours ago and you didn't tell me?'

There was a loud tut behind them. Reuben shook his head and turned, giving a smile to the elderly woman behind him who was looking at him as if he'd just run over her cat.

He lifted his hand towards Lara. 'I thought you might be upset.'

The colour in her cheeks was building. If he'd thought her eyes had been lasers before, now they were definitely shooting sparks.

He was surprised by how cute she was when she was angry.

'I guess I was right,' he said, as he picked up his coffee and drained his cup.

Lara's fists were clenched on the tabletop. It took a few seconds for the blanched knuckles to be gently released and Lara sagged down into her chair.

'All my things…gone?' she asked.

He nodded his head. This was what he'd wanted to avoid. Her shoulders slumped and the high colour in her cheeks started to disperse, replaced with a white pallor.

She blinked. Oh, no. Her eyes were getting that sheeny way—the way they did before a woman burst into tears.

She started murmuring. 'But what am I going to do? That was my entire summer wardrobe.' She shook her head. 'I have nothing—not a single thing to take with me on the cruise.' One fat, hot tear spilled down her cheek. 'And I certainly didn't budget for this.'

She took a deep, ragged kind of breath. She was twisting a napkin between her fingers. 'It's not just the clothes. I had other things in that case. Things that meant a lot to me. Things I can't replace.' Her voice was getting shakier as she spoke.

'What kind of things?' He could feel the march of a thousand cold feet down his spine. What else had Josh flung out to the trash?

'There…there was something special.' A tear rolled down her cheek.

'What was it?'

She shook her head and brushed away the tear. 'It was nothing. It wasn't valuable. Just a keepsake. Something I've had since childhood.'

He was curious now. It must have been something special for her to be reacting this way. He reached over and touched her hand.

She gulped. 'It's silly, really. It was a book. A copy of *Alice in Wonderland*. My gran bought it for me when I was little. We used to read it all the time. And it doesn't matter that I could walk into any bookshop and buy another copy. It wouldn't be this one. The one we read for hours.'

Reuben spoke quietly. 'And it was in the case with the summer clothes?'

He shouldn't just have held Josh against the wall. He should have done much, much worse.

She gave a little nod. 'I just can't bear the thought I won't see it again.' She pressed her hand against her heart. 'It was full of memories for me. Every time I opened the pages again I thought about my gran. She died just after I'd been accepted for university.'

Something clicked in his brain. 'And you didn't go?'

Lara bit her lip. It was obvious she was thinking about how to reply. He didn't do this. He didn't form emotional attachments with women. He didn't like tears and sniffles. It was his first cue to walk away.

Or his first cue to do his natural alternative—throw money at a situation.

He reached across the table and grabbed Lara's hand. 'Come on.' He pulled her to her feet and started walking.

He could sense she could barely keep with his long strides but he didn't want to think about that too much.

'Reuben, where are we going?' she sniffed.

For some reason he couldn't even bear to look at her. Here was a woman he barely knew—but he couldn't stand to see her upset. It did strange things to his brain. Strange things to his equilibrium. And he couldn't quite fathom why.

This wasn't his fault. None of it was his fault, but that wasn't helping.

There was one thing he could do here—one thing that he had. The thing that seemed the quickest fix for most people in the world. Money.

CHAPTER FIVE

LARA COULD FEEL panic begin to set in. Where on earth could she get some money? She had a tiny bit of spending money for the cruise, put away every month and hidden in an account that Josh had known nothing about. She'd hoped it would cover the gratuity charge for the trip and whatever drinks package she wanted to buy. She'd pre-paid a few excursions when she'd booked the trip and had thought she wouldn't need much more money.

If only she'd known.

She cringed, putting her head between her hands. Five weeks ago she'd bought a pink dress with tiny glittery beads. More money than she'd ever spent on one item. But it had practically called out to her from the shop window. And it was perfect for a cruise. And she'd had the rest of her wardrobe—or so she'd thought.

She started to think frantically. Borrow. She could borrow clothes. But who from? One of her best friends was in Australia and the other in the US. She had a couple of acquaintances in London but none of them were the same size as her.

She started fingering the edge of her jacket. There was a whole wardrobe full of clothes upstairs in the house. She'd already borrowed a nightdress from Addison—but that had been an emergency situation. There was no way she could let herself borrow any of Addison's clothes. They were way out of her league. And what if she damaged something? How on earth would she replace it?

She swallowed. Her mouth was dry. She could do with some water. She could feel herself starting to panic. Control. It was slipping away from her just when she'd thought she could capture it back. Josh had been quite controlling. Comments about her hair, her make-up and her clothes. She'd tried to ignore them, but after more than a year together he'd chipped away at her self-confidence. Now, just when she thought she could shake him off, he'd done something else to control her. This wasn't just about the clothes. It was about taking back charge of her life.

Reuben had ushered her into a lift. She hadn't been paying attention but the doors swished open right in the heart of the designer womenswear section. Right now she couldn't even afford to buy a pair of sunglasses—not when her finances were in such dire straits.

Reuben was still muttering into his phone. It was obvious from the expression on his face and his tone that he wasn't the slightest bit happy.

His eyes flickered towards her and he gave a start as he realised the lift doors had opened. 'I'm busy,' he hissed into the phone, jamming it back in his pocket.

Lara couldn't even think straight. Her head was still full of every item of clothing that she'd need to replace with unknown funds so by the time he'd steered her in and out of the lift she didn't have a clue where she was.

An elegant young woman in a dark suit with a jaunty scarf at her neck greeted them. 'Mr Tyler?' she asked. 'I'm Bree, your personal shopper.'

Reuben nodded, his hand firmly in the small of Lara's back. 'This is my friend, Lara Callaway,' he said swiftly. 'She's had a mishap with her summer wardrobe and needs some replacements.' He glanced around the dazzling array of clothes. 'Things that will be suitable for a summer cruise she'll be enjoying in a couple of weeks.'

This time Lara did blink. She was trying to suck in a breath between her tightly clenched lips.

The dark-haired, red-lipped woman nodded attentively. She was so neat. So tidy. So professional that Lara felt entirely dowdy. But Bree nodded as if she were the most important person on the planet and steered her towards a room. 'What kind of things would you like? Dresses? Skirts? Or trousers? Is there a particular colour you prefer? And would you like daywear as well as nightwear?'

Lara felt herself nod along and murmur, 'Pink, or blue, or green. Any summer colours really.' How come she already knew that Bree had that ruthless efficiency edge to her personality type?

Her hands pressed self-consciously against her stomach. 'Do you need to know my size?'

Bree shook her head, her eyes running up and down her body. 'No problem. I've got your size,' she said confidently. She ushered Lara behind a set of velvet curtains. 'Get undressed and I'll be back in a few minutes.'

Reuben hadn't even lifted his head from his phone. He was answering some text or email as he sat down in the velvet-covered chair in the corner of the room.

Another assistant appeared with some glasses and a bottle of champagne. She poured them without a word and set one glass down on the table next to Reuben and the other in the dressing room next to Lara. 'Would you like some chocolates?'

Lara shook her head wordlessly. If she couldn't afford a cup of tea in here, she certainly couldn't afford any clothes.

She stood behind the curtains and stared out at Reuben for a few seconds. He looked furious. She was almost scared to speak.

She grabbed hold of the edge of one of the purple velvet curtains. 'Reuben,' she hissed.

He didn't even acknowledge that she'd spoken.

She tried again. 'Reuben!' This time she was louder. He looked up.

'What?'

She blinked back the tears that were threatening to fill her eyes again. 'Why did you bring me here? I can't afford any of this stuff.' Her stomach clenched. 'You should have told me. You should have told me about my clothes this morning. Then I might have had a chance to get something sorted instead of wasting time over coffee and cakes!'

He frowned. 'What are you worrying about? I'll cover the cost of your clothes.' He waved his hand and went back to his email.

Her mouth fell open. 'What? No.' She couldn't believe it. Why would someone she barely knew offer to restock her wardrobe for her?

He gave a little shrug as he kept bashing away at his phone.

She opened her mouth to speak but Bree swept back into the private changing room with half the contents of the store held effortlessly over her arm.

She stood behind the curtains with Lara and systematically hung things up. 'You're not ready yet?' she asked as everything was slotted into place. 'Summer dresses, skirts and matching tops, Capri pants and a variety of matching items. You get started and I'll find some eveningwear for you and some shoes.' She regarded the rainbow of clothes hanging in front of her nose. 'I've brought the colours I thought would suit you best, but we can change that if there's anything you don't particularly like.'

She swept back out without another word and Lara gulped. She wasn't sure she'd have the heart to tell Bree she didn't like anything she'd chosen.

She stared down at her skinny jeans, brown boots and simple top. Talk about being out of place.

She picked up the glass of champagne and stared at it for a second before taking a nervous gulp. Bree wasn't making her uncomfortable. She'd been nothing but efficient. Lara was making herself uncomfortable.

She fingered one of the pale pink summer dresses hanging in front of her. It was gorgeous and would suit her pale complexion and blonde hair perfectly. But there was no way she was even looking at the price tag.

Where was the harm in trying on a few nice things? There was no way she'd let Reuben buy them for her, but on an ordinary day she would never dare to come in here and try on all these clothes. It was a bit like being a child in a sweetie shop, surrounded by a million fabulous sweeties crammed in jars all around her.

She kicked off her boots and jeans, leaving them in a rumpled heap on the floor, tossing her T-shirt on top. It took only a few seconds to slip the dress over her shoulders and slide the zip into place. She stood back a little to get a look in the mirror.

That was what a dress that probably cost more than her monthly salary looked like.

Nice. More than nice. She ran the palms over the fabric. Gorgeous.

The curtain moved behind her and Bree appeared at her elbow. 'Oh…very nice,' she said, as she deposited some glittering eveningwear on the hooks on the wall. 'Step outside and get a proper look. The light is better there.'

Bree swept back the curtain before Lara had a chance to object. The noise attracted Reuben's attention and he looked up. There was a slight rise of his eyebrows. 'Very Monte Carlo,' he quipped.

She wasn't used to having a guy around while she tried on clothes. Parts of her favourite movie were springing to mind. On one hand it brought a smile to her face, and on the other she was feeling slightly uncomfortable.

She stepped in front of one of the other mirrors. It was a gorgeous dress. Perfect for sitting in the café opposite the Casino in Monte Carlo. Oh, she already had her whole visit planned out.

Bree held up another summer dress. This one was pale yellow dotted with tiny flowers—not dissimilar to a top she owned. 'Try this one too,' she urged. 'I think it will look just as nice and be a good contrast for you.' She gave a wave of her hand. 'I'll get you some sandals.' She wrinkled her nose. 'Will you be doing any walking?'

Lara nodded. 'I expect to be doing lots of walking.'

Bree nodded. 'I'll get you some wedges, then.' She disappeared again and Lara stared over at Reuben. She might as well not exist right now. He was talking on the phone again. Someone was getting the benefit of his full attention—but she wasn't entirely sure she wanted that to change.

She took a few steps back and her hands settled at the edge of the velvet curtains—it was almost as if she was peeking around at him.

From here she was beginning to get the whole 'bad boy' experience. Trouble was, it was making her blood rush quicker around her body. The skin at the back of her neck prickled as he started full-on ranting at the person at the end of the phone. He'd taken off his jacket and laid it across another chair, giving her a bird's-eye view of the muscles rippling underneath the thin fabric of his T-shirt.

There was a hint of stubble along his jaw line and even from here—at the other side of the room—she could see his dark brown eyes blazing. She ducked back behind the curtain and wriggled her way out of the pink dress, taking the yellow one off the hanger. It really was cute, she liked it, she could imagine herself standing in front of the Leaning Tower in this dress and taking a photo. Right now she would be standing in front of the Leaning Tower in her underwear. She shook her head and took another little gulp of her drink. Too quick, and this time the bubbles shot up her nose, making her cough and splutter.

A head appeared around the curtain followed by a warm hand that thudded her back.

'Reuben!' she gasped as she held the dress up in front of herself.

It was no use. He had a rear view anyway and from his amused expression he was taking full advantage.

'What?' Even though the word was innocent, with his Irish accent it sounded like pure cheek.

'Get out!' she hissed.

He disappeared back behind the curtain and she pulled on the dress as quickly as she could, yanking back the curtains, ready to tell him exactly what she thought.

Bree breezed back into the room with two pairs of wedges in each hand. Her footsteps faltered and she looked from one to the other.

Lara was mad but Reuben was sitting with his arms folded, one leg slung over the other with a look of pure amusement on his face.

'Should I come back?' Bree asked hesitantly.

'Don't mind me.' He shrugged.

'I thought you were on the phone,' Lara snapped.

He shrugged again. 'I was. That was round one.' He glanced at his watch. 'I'd say round two will start in about five minutes. Let's see how much you can try on in that space of time.'

He stood up and walked over to her, flooding her with a waft of his aftershave. 'The dress is perfect for you.' He looked towards Bree and pointed at the wedges. 'And I like the natural-coloured ones. Not so plastic looking. Get them.'

His phone buzzed in his pocket and he ignored it. He

looked at the huge amount of clothing hanging from the hooks. 'What else do you like?'

She was stunned. She wasn't quite sure what to make of this. There was no way on this planet that Reuben Tyler was the least bit interested in women's clothes. Not unless he was removing them. What was he playing at?

Bree was smiling anxiously behind him. It would be rude not to respond. She ran her hand down some of the items hanging in front of her. 'I like this one, and this one. Not so much that one or that one.' She pulled out a pair of white Capri pants. 'I still need to try these on.'

Reuben's eyes fixed on something else, and his hand brushed across hers as he reached between the clothes and pulled out something shimmering underneath. It was a gold evening dress. Almost invisible net fabric covered in tiny gold sequins and jewels adorned with fringes— almost like a really chic flapper-style dress.

He held it up against her. 'I think this will really suit you.'

She gulped. It was gorgeous but she could tell from just looking it was way out of price range. On a normal day she'd be too scared to even touch a dress like this.

She shook her head. 'It's probably too fancy for a cruise ship.' Her voice came out almost as a squeak.

Reuben's phone sounded in his pocket again. He completely ignored it, his eyes fixed firmly on hers. He leaned forward, the stubble at the side of his jaw scraping her cheek as he whispered in her ear, 'Go on, try it on. For me.' He stood back.

Bree was wide-eyed behind him. 'I have the perfect sandals for that dress,' she said quietly, before turning on her heel and disappearing.

It was weird, the effect he was having on her skin. Was it the voice? The smell? Or just the masculinity that seemed to exude from his pores? A million little butterflies were currently beating their wings against her skin, making her unable to focus on anything else.

It didn't help that she couldn't seem to draw her eyes away from his hypnotic gaze. Those deep brown eyes just kept pulling her in and she felt her body drift towards his almost subconsciously. And his was moving too, as if pulled by an invisible magnet. His hand caught at the back of her head, tangling in her hair.

She had a wave of déjà vu. Back to earlier in the café downstairs. Back to the feel of his lips against hers. Back to feeling stunned when they'd finally pulled away.

'These ones! I told you they were per...' Bree's voice tailed off as both parties jumped back.

Reuben muttered a curse under his breath and stalked back over to the chair. Lara tried to suck in the air around her but that was a bad idea. Because all she inhaled in was the remnants of his aftershave and that did funny things to her ability to concentrate. She made a grab for the shoes. 'Thanks.' And whipped the curtain closed in front of the stunned Bree's face before sagging against the mirror.

She squeezed her eyes closed. It could have been so much worse. They could have actually been kissing. Come to think of it, she was quite sure people had been caught in much more compromising positions than they had in these fitting rooms.

Something coiled inside her. Something odd. She might be feeling a little off balance but part of her felt cheated. Cheated out of what might actually have come next.

Her hand went automatically to the glass but it was already empty. Her throat had never felt so dry but the last thing she should do right now was ask for more. It had obviously gone to her head already.

She peered round the curtain to locate Bree. 'Could I trouble you for a glass of still water, please?'

Bree nodded and disappeared, leaving Lara with a few seconds to try and think straight.

She took a deep breath and looked at the dress again. It was gorgeous. Better than she could ever have imagined. Reuben had asked to see her in it, and how wrong was it to play princess for five minutes?

The dress slipped over her shoulders as if it had been made just for her. It covered everything but gave the illusion of not quite covering everything at all. The gold jewelled sandals did match perfectly, with just enough of a heel to give her some elegance without having the fear of falling on her face.

Her hand toyed with the curtain. She loved it. But what would Reuben think—and why on earth was that important?

She pulled the curtain back and stepped out into the room. The brighter lights in the larger room caught the beadwork, sequins and fringes on her dress, sending little shards of colour scattering all around the room.

The rainbow effect made Reuben look up from his phone. His eyes widened and his tongue ran slowly along his lower lip. 'Oh, wow...' His voice was low and throaty.

Bree reappeared with the glass of water in her hand. 'Gorgeous,' she breathed.

He waved his hand towards Bree without taking his eyes off Lara. 'This one's definitely a keeper.'

She was caught. She loved this dress. She loved everything about it. But it was just a dream. Like the rest of the clothes behind the curtain. A dream that could never be hers.

'We'll take it.' He'd lost his huskiness. Now his voice was determined.

'What? No. No, we can't. I don't even know how much it costs.' *And probably don't want to know, because that would definitely spoil the dream.*

'It doesn't matter. I'd said I'd cover it. That...' he glanced down at her bare legs '...and the shoes. And the rest of the clothes she tried on and liked.' He walked back over to the range of clothes and picked up a slinky electric-blue dress. 'I like this one too, it matches your eyes. Try it on and if you like it we'll have it too.' He nodded towards a bright pink dress with sparkling circular beads. 'And that one.'

He punched a number into his phone and put it to his ear.

Bree started flapping around her, a wide smile reaching from ear to ear. She lifted out the clothes that Lara had preferred. 'Okay, I'll put these ones over here.' She pointed to the capri pants and blue dress. 'Take your time and try those on too. I've got a gorgeous pink printed blouse that will match those pants.' She disappeared before Lara had a chance to speak again.

Lara looked down. It would be so easy right now to say yes. But she couldn't. She just couldn't. She didn't want to feel as if she owed anything to Reuben. And it didn't matter that he didn't give her that vibe—money was no object to a man like him. She just didn't want to feel like that.

Reuben's voice started to rise. 'That's enough. You have a responsibility to the club. If you renege on the deal now it could affect the club's shares.'

Lara was hesitating behind the curtain. It didn't look like now was a good time to talk to Reuben. She shifted from foot to foot then grabbed the white capri pants and tried them on. Bree was back a few seconds later with the printed pink shirt.

Bree's taste was impeccable. She hadn't picked a single thing that hadn't complemented Lara's skin tone and shape. The pink shirt was printed with little birds and tied at the front. It was perfect.

Bree gave a little sigh. 'That's fantastic. Is there anything else I can get you?'

'No.' Lara said the words quickly before she could change her mind. This was getting out of hand.

She slid the shirt and pants back off and handed them to Bree, who disappeared while she pulled her skinny jeans and T-shirt on again. She pulled back the curtain as she tugged on her boots and shouted over to Reuben. 'Reuben, we really need to talk.'

He glanced up from his phone and waved his hand at her. This was getting old.

She marched over in front of him. It was clear he was mad. His voice had risen even more and now he was just plain shouting. 'I'm tired of this. Fed up having to try and placate an adult who is acting like a two-year-old. Enough! I'm done dealing with you.' He hung up and jammed his phone in his pocket as his other hand kneaded the side of his temple.

If Reuben had been in the same room as that player he would probably have killed him with his bare hands. Troubleshooting was becoming exasperating. This one footballer had signed for a lesser-known club, taken part in the announcements and then decided to back out of the deal—after the club's shares had already soared and they'd spent a huge amount of funds on printing his name across their shirts. Kids were already fighting to get one.

The player's temper tantrum and bad behaviour could bankrupt a club that had already been on the brink.

He blinked and looked up. Lara was standing in front of him with her hands on her hips. His stomach did that crazy thing it had in the last few hours and flipped over. She'd been the one bright thing in the past twenty-four hours.

'What?'

She shook her head. 'You can't buy those clothes for me.' She held out her hands. 'Reuben, I shouldn't even be in a place like this. I probably can't afford a bra from this place, let alone anything else.'

'You need a bra?' That was creating pictures in his mind it shouldn't. Every time they'd appeared in his brain these last few hours he'd tried to force his memories back to the pink onesie. That usually killed any hormones plain dead.

Lara's brow creased into a frown. 'No. I don't need a bra. I need to be able to pay for my own clothes.'

He stared at her. 'Why?'

Lara threw up her hands and stared at him in disbelief. 'Why? *Why?* Because I hardly know you. Because these clothes are for me, not you. Because I like to walk around in things that I've bought with money that I've *earned.* Because it's important to me to be independent.'

He didn't get it. Not really. Every other woman he'd ever dealt with loved it when he threw money at them.

He gave a little smile. 'But you looked beautiful in the clothes. They'd be perfect for the cruise.'

Her shoulders sagged. 'I know that. But I can't afford them. And it's important for me to be able to look after myself.'

Okay. Maybe she was making sense. He'd thought this was an easy get-out clause after not telling her about her disposed-of summer wardrobe.

His phone rang again and he flinched. A wave of concern washed over her face and she reached over and took his hand, her argument about money momentarily forgotten. 'You know what? Maybe you need to think about something else. You've spent an hour constantly fighting with that guy on the phone. When was the last time *you* had a holiday?'

That was easy. 'Spring. Four years ago. My dad was in hospital.'

'You haven't had a holiday in four years? That's ridiculous. It's about time you had a break.'

He shook his head. Ugh. Bad idea. 'Breaks don't make you money. I don't do holidays. They're a waste of time.'

She let out a laugh. 'I guess you and I have different priorities. My holiday is the one thing I look forward to every year.' Her voice tailed off and she looked outside the dressing room.

There it was again. That expression on her face. The one that made him feel like the worst person in the world. He hated it when she looked like that. It didn't matter that none of this was really his fault. His only crime had been his act of omission. But he still didn't like the fact that right now he'd do anything to take that look off her face.

A tiny seed was starting to sprout in his brain. Lara was looking up at him with those clear blue eyes. What on earth had that clown Josh been thinking? The guy must have had rocks in his head.

She was shaking her head again, glancing over her shoulder to make sure Bree wasn't around. 'This was a nice idea, Reuben. It really was.' She ran her hand over her own skinny jeans. 'But it can't happen. This…today… It was a bit like being a fairy princess for an hour or so. But time's up. It's back to real life and the fact I'll probably need to raid some of the second-hand shops to see if I can restock my summer wardrobe.'

He tried to interrupt but she held up her hand. 'Don't. I don't want charity—and I know you don't mean it like that. I know you're just trying to do something nice.' She gave him a rueful smile and pressed her hand against her heart. 'But your something nice makes me feel bad in here. It makes me feel as if I can't look after myself. It makes me feel as if I need someone to bail me out.' She shook her head. 'I don't want to feel like that. I *can't* feel like that right now. Finding Josh in bed with someone else is doing enough damage to my self-esteem right now. You need to let me find my own way with this too.' She stood up. This time her flat abdomen was right in front of his face.

It was probably an unwitting action. She reached out with her hand and ran her fingers through his hair. 'Come on, Reuben, let's get out of here before your favourite footballer calls back and you spontaneously combust.'

As if by magic his phone buzzed in his pocket again and he could feel his rage rising. He'd spent the last few years working non-stop. For the most part he'd liked it. It wasn't as if he had a wife and child to come home to and the lifestyle suited him. He loved the energy of his job, even thrived on the stress a little, but the last day had made him stop to breathe for a moment.

When was the last time he'd taken a holiday? When was the last time he'd even *thought* about taking a holiday?

He'd always had a take-no-prisoners attitude and it had served him well in his line of work, which was full of inflated egos. He called things as he saw them and worked hard for any team he dealt with. But now? If he had five minutes alone in a room with the current diva he was dealing with it was likely he'd do something he shouldn't.

The truth was he needed some time out. He needed some time away.

He stood up quickly, his hand catching Lara's waist.

She didn't flinch, just wrapped her hand over his and moved a little closer, putting her other hand on his shoulder. 'You okay?'

He could hear the genuine concern in her voice. Her light floral perfume with tinges of orange was floating up around him. She brushed her hand against his cheek.

The unanswered phone buzzed again and Lara let out a sigh of exasperation. She dipped into the pocket of his jeans, retrieved the phone and pressed the button. 'Reuben Tyler is unavailable to take your call,' she said sharply.

After a few seconds her eyebrows rose. The footballer was obviously on a tirade. She shot Reuben a cheeky smile as she shook her head. 'Finished?' she enquired into the phone. 'In that case, the answers to your questions were no, no and no. And don't call us, we'll call you.' She hung up and put his phone in her bag.

He'd never actually had anyone take charge of him before. It was a whole new experience. Lara just shrugged. 'I didn't like him much.' She started heading towards the door. 'You should make yourself unavailable for a while until he sorts himself out.'

She was so matter-of-fact about it. Her head wasn't thumping with stocks, shares and the livelihoods of everyone attached to the club. It was almost like a light-bulb moment for him.

He followed her out to the main department, wincing at the bright lights. Bree was standing behind the nearest counter with a whole range of beautifully folded clothes, awaiting payment.

Lara's footsteps faltered. 'Oh, no,' she whispered.

He walked right into the back of her and slid his hand around her waist. 'Don't panic. I have the perfect solution.'

She spun around to face him, her lips just inches from his. It struck him that to anyone looking they must appear a couple. 'Does she work on commission?' Lara whispered. 'Have I just ruined her entire day?'

He reached for his wallet. 'I'm going to pay.'

She grabbed hold of his hand. 'No, Reuben. We've spoken about this.'

He gave her a smile. 'Not entirely. I'm paying you back.'

She frowned. 'Paying me back for what?'

He waved his hand and stopped Bree from wrapping

the pink dress. 'Here,' he said with a flourish. 'Go and put that back on.'

'Why on earth would I do that?'

'I'll let you know what I'm paying you back for once we get out of here. Let's test-drive your fancy new clothes.'

She was bewildered. But Reuben had already swiped his credit card. Bree reached behind her and pulled the silver sandals back out of the bag. 'Here, take these too. You can change back in the dressing room.'

Lara held the glittering pink dress in her hand. Was she finally losing her mind? Maybe this was all just some crazy dream and any second now she'd wake up and find out the last few days hadn't happened at all.

The bright lights of the shop made the dress glitter even more. It was gorgeous. It was a beautiful dress. She'd actually looked at herself in the mirror and held her breath.

She shrugged. Where was the harm in this? It was only temporary. Most of the clothes she could still return. The pink dress?

Well, that might just be destiny.

The bar was beautiful. In one of the most well-known five-star hotels in London, it was sleek, chic and discreet. It was definitely the place to bring a date you wanted to impress. The opulent art deco setting couldn't be any sexier—smouldering black lacquer, burnished gold alcoves, velvet upholstery and the kind of low lighting that showed off everyone to their best advantage.

Normally Lara would have shied away from a place like this, but with her shimmering pink designer dress and silver sandals, for once she didn't feel out of place.

Reuben obviously knew the cocktail bar well. He nodded to the barman and handed her a cocktail menu. 'What would you like?'

She was too busy staring at the chandelier directly above her head. She gave a shrug. 'Something fruity.'

He shook his head and leaned across the bar to place an order. 'What do you think of the place?'

She glanced around at all the elegant couples in the room. They looked like they did this every day. 'It's beautiful,' she said quietly. 'Very elegant.'

Reuben pointed over to the corner. 'Over there? That's the former cabaret stage where George Gershwin and Frank Sinatra performed.'

She sucked in her breath as the barman slid some orange-coloured drinks towards them. The drinks were just as glamorous as the place. Served in stunning, long-stemmed crystal glassware, she was almost too afraid to even take a sip.

The peach-flavoured icy drink was delicious. A few more of these and she would drift off into a world all of her own. And from where she was currently sitting, she would take the sexy Irish man right with her.

No. She shook her head. Silly thoughts. Ridiculous thoughts. It was just…she couldn't stop focusing on those lips. Those lips that had kissed her earlier like she'd never been kissed before. Was that what kisses were meant to be like? How come it had taken this long for her to find out?

She took another sip of the peach cocktail. It was gorgeous, just the right amount of sweetness with a little bit of tartness. It was so easy to get carried away in a place like this, with its decadence and splendour. Particularly when she was dressed like this and had the handsomest man in the room on her arm. It was almost like being in a movie. Time for a reality check.

She owed Reuben a huge amount of money. And in spite of the glamour and ambience of a place like this, that made her feel distinctly uncomfortable. He didn't give her controlling vibes at all. But she wanted to be in charge of her own life. She wanted every decision she made to be based only on what she wanted—no more outside influences. She really needed to clear the air about this before she could move forward. And there was no time like the present.

She looked over at him and took a deep breath. 'So, tell me, Reuben. How am I going to pay you back?'

Reuben was relaxed. He was feeling chilled. And it was the first time he'd felt like this in weeks—perhaps months.

Lara looked absolutely stunning. She'd pulled her blonde hair up in some kind of silver clasp, leaving little tendrils around her ears. She'd found some pink lipstick somewhere and it matched her dress to perfection. She looked as if she'd spent all day getting ready when the reality was he knew it had only taken ten minutes.

Another thing he liked about her. Along with a whole host of others.

He couldn't understand why she wasn't more confident about herself. It was one of the reasons he'd suggested she test-drive her new clothes. He'd known just how stunning she looked in them. And so did every other guy in the room. All eyes had been on Lara from the second they'd walked in here. Only she didn't seem to notice.

It had come to him in a blinding flash exactly how he should play this. There was chemistry between them. No one could deny it. And after one taste of her lips he was sure he wanted to taste a whole lot more.

He got it that she was proud. He got it that she didn't want a handout. And while he admired that—and he certainly wasn't used to it—it put him in a bit of a difficult position.

Then she'd made the suggestion herself. Reuben should have a holiday.

The idea had never appealed before.

But the idea had never had a blonde-haired, pink-dressed beautiful woman dangling before his eyes. Maybe a quick fling would get Lara Callaway out of his system?

Sure, Caleb might kill him. But from where he was standing it would be worth it.

More than worth it.

And maybe some time together would instil a little more confidence into this gorgeous woman? Maybe, if she had the holiday she'd always dreamed of, and didn't have to worry about money, she'd be able to see herself the way he saw her. A sexy, gorgeous woman with the world at her feet.

She was still waiting for him to answer as she sipped at her straw through those delectable lips.

'That's easy.' He gave her one of his dazzling smiles. 'You'll pay me back by letting me go on the cruise with you.'

She blinked, then her brow furrowed. 'Wait a minute. I'm lost. Want to run this by me again?'

Maybe he should buy her another cocktail. 'It's simple. You told me I need to take a holiday, and you don't want me to pay to replace your clothes. This is the easy solution. I come on the cruise with you—and instead of refunding your cash for my share, I buy you a new wardrobe.' He let his eyes roam up and down her body in the glittering pink dress. Boy, did she wear it well. 'That way you don't feel indebted to me because you're officially buying your own clothes.'

She made a noise. Maybe it was a whimper. 'But... but...' The words just wouldn't form. 'But you don't do holidays,' she finally squeaked.

He lifted one eyebrow. 'It seems like I do now.'

She lifted up her hands. 'But you hardly know me.'

She looked panicked and it made the edges of his

mouth curl up in amusement. 'Then clearly that's about to change.'

She wasn't talking. Her mouth was hanging open. It was the first time he'd really seen Lara lost for words. It made him want to laugh.

He walked smoothly behind her, pressing his chest against her shoulders and looking into the glass in the gantry ahead of them. He bent down and whispered in her ear.

'Stop panicking, Lara. Let the rational side of your brain kick in for a few seconds.'

She was staring straight ahead, watching their reflections in the glass gantry. It was the first time he'd really seen them together—seen what the rest of the world must see when they looked at them.

He smiled. He was absolutely doing the right thing. Two weeks on a cruise with this woman? He'd have to be crazy to let her go alone.

She was staring right back. Watching him, with his head at her shoulder and his arm slipping around her waist. She still looked pretty stunned.

'You know it makes sense,' he said smoothly. 'Technically, you're paying for your own clothes. I'm just refunding you for the half of the cruise that I'll be taking in Josh's place.'

It seemed almost reasonable. If she jumbled it around in her head for long enough she could find arguments and counter-arguments everywhere.

The cruise was days away.

She really, really wanted to go.

And she really needed something to wear.

Did she want to spend two weeks on a cruise ship alone?

None of this was normal. None of this was rational. That kiss must have driven her crazy because she couldn't think a single sensible thought.

She took a huge sip of her cocktail. 'Okay,' she said quickly, as she felt his fingers at her waist. She lifted her cocktail glass towards him. 'Two weeks on the cruise of a lifetime.'

Reuben walked around to her side and picked up his glass. His fingers hadn't left her waist. He clinked his glass against hers. The look on his face was almost predatory.

He gave her a wicked smile. 'My first holiday in four years. This could be fun.'

CHAPTER SIX

LARA HADN'T STOPPED chattering for the last thirty minutes. All the way on the transfer from the airport to the cruise-ship terminal.

Reuben pushed his credit card towards the red-lipped hostess who'd just given them the hard sell. 'Yes to the drinks package and yes to the excursion package.'

The woman beamed at them both and swiped his card in the blink of an eye.

'Reuben,' hissed Lara. 'That's probably way more expensive that it ought to be. I'd already prepaid a few excursions.'

He shook his head and put his arm behind her back, pressing gently to urge her to move forward. He wasn't going to argue about this. 'Why come on a cruise and only go on a few excursions? Let's just enjoy them all.' The ship was gleaming next to them.

'Didn't you say you wanted to do the excursions to Monaco, Rome and Pisa?'

She nodded.

'And don't you think it's likely we'll drink a couple of glasses of wine with dinner each day?'

She pressed her lips together and nodded again.

He gave her back a little push again towards the embarkation point. Her footsteps faltered as she tried to push her passport back in her bag. Her hands were trembling.

He blinked. Over in the corner of the room a child was jumping up and down with excitement. Another couple—

clearly on their honeymoon—kept stopping on the gang-way to take pictures. The whole check-in hall was buzzing.

He hadn't been on a holiday in so long that he'd forgotten about the build-up and the expectations. Last time he'd gone on holiday a few years ago he'd booked a flight and hotel and had left later that day. Nothing had been planned.

But according to Lara she'd planned this for years. She'd wanted to go on a cruise ship since she was a child and after finally saving up the money had spent weeks choosing between different cruise liners and itineraries. No wonder she was nervous. It was kind of cute.

He stopped her in front of the ship. 'Wait a minute. Let's take your picture before you board.'

She gave him a smile as she glanced up at the gleaming hull. For the next two weeks four thousand passengers would live in a different world, leaving one port at night and waking up in another. Would not have to worry about making breakfast, lunch or dinner and be able to choose between relaxing on board or visiting a different city every day.

On paper it actually sounded quite good. The reality of being trapped on a ship with four thousand people he might not actually like for a fortnight gave him a whole host of other thoughts.

Lara pulled her sunglasses down from her head. She was wearing the sunny yellow dress and wedges. It suited her—complimenting her long legs—even though he'd noticed her pulling it down a few times. He lifted up his phone. 'Smile. We finally got here. You're about to have the holiday of a lifetime.'

Her smile wavered for a second and he could see her take a deep breath. She'd spent the last two days in a complete flurry. To be frank, he was surprised they'd even got here. He'd never known anyone double-check on twenty occasions that they had their passports, tickets, itineraries and boarding passes. He snapped the picture quickly. 'Come on,' he said. 'Let's get on board before they leave without us.'

His hand was at the small of her back again. Although her summer dress covered every part of her, the fabric was thin and she could feel the warmth from his palm. It didn't matter that the summer sun was scorching down on her shoulders and face, all she could concentrate on was the heat at the base of her spine.

All the crew were impeccably dressed in white and nodded and greeted each of the guests in turn.

The main reception area of the cruise ship had a central open space, right up the middle of the ship, with a grand piano at the bottom with a curved bar. Lara let out a squeal when she saw the stairs. 'Look, Reuben, they've got crystals in them. Aren't they gorgeous?'

He was obviously amused at her delight. 'Want your picture taken on the stairs?'

She glanced down at her dress. 'Should I wait until I'm wearing one of the evening dresses?'

'Why don't we take a picture in every outfit?' The easy smile he gave her sent little ripples up her spine. She could see a few other guests smile at his accent. Sex appeal just dripped from this man.

'Sure, why not?'

It was odd. At Addison's house in London she'd been comfortable around Reuben. When the two of them were in the house together there was definite underlying current. But it was pleasant. It made the air around them buzz.

But here—somewhere new—the buzz felt a little different. Sparkier. More sexual. Maybe it was because she could see other people reacting to the man she was with. Maybe it was because she was officially on holiday and was just excited by the cruise. But she had a sneaking suspicion it was more to do with the man, rather than the place.

There was something more restrictive about being under the roof of her employer and Reuben's friend. Here, there was no one to answer to. No one to catch them doing something they shouldn't.

Where had that come from?

Reuben had pressed the button for the glass elevator and gestured her over. 'Let's check out the cabin then we can go up on deck and grab a drink for the cast off.'

The elevator slid up smoothly to their floor and they walked along to their cabin. Part of the expense of the trip had been her superior cabin selection, larger than average with a balcony she intended to sit on every night.

But the number of this cabin corresponded with a higher floor. She was curious.

He slid the card they'd received at check-in into the door as her stomach flip-flopped over. And it nearly flip-flopped over onto her new wedges.

This wasn't a cabin—it was a suite.

The place was stunning. A deep red carpet covered the floor of what looked like a sitting room. There was a huge comfortable sofa and a large-screen TV fixed on the wall. One side of the room didn't have a wall—it was pure full-length glass windows with a balcony running along the length of the cabin giving spectacular views.

She almost couldn't speak. 'Great,' said Reuben, walking easily across the room to the small bar in the corner. Her feet carried her forward. The first door on her right led to the bathroom. Second on the right was the bedroom. Now she nearly did fall over.

One enormous king-sized bed took up most of the room.

'I phoned them,' she said quickly. 'I phoned them to ask for it to be changed to two beds.' She spun around and held out her hands. 'And this can't possibly be ours. I didn't pay for a suite—just a superior cabin. There must have been some mistake.'

Reuben didn't blink, just strode over and jumped on the bed, lying back amongst the array of pillows with his arms behind his head. 'No mistake. I paid to upgrade us. Figured we might as well do this in style.' He gave her a wink. 'As for the bed, I don't mind if you don't.'

Her feet were frozen to the floor as her stomach tumbled over. This wasn't supposed to happen. Of course she'd booked a king-size bed when she'd thought she'd been coming on the cruise with rat boyfriend. But as soon as Reuben had suggested he come along instead, she'd amended her booking.

'Let…let me go and speak to the concierge,' she stumbled. 'Maybe they could put two beds in here instead?'

Reuben rolled on his side, head on his hand, facing towards her. 'Why bother? Look at the view you've got from that balcony. What if the only other cabin is down in the bowels of the ship? No view. No balcony. I imagine a cruise like this is pretty much booked out.'

She swallowed. He was probably right. But surely it couldn't hurt to check?

He propped himself up a little further. 'Look at the view we have of Venice right now. Imagine coming into port at Barcelona and getting to see the whole city. And what about Monte Carlo? There'd be a view of the race track, the casino and all the mountains.'

He was right. She knew he was right. But the thought of sharing a bed with Reuben Tyler was doing strange things to her senses. It was almost as if his woody aftershave, laced with pheromones, was snaking its way across the room to her like a big lasso. If this was how it was just being in the same room, what would it be like sharing a bed?

She knew it. She should have brought the onesie.

And he was relishing every second of her uncomfortable squirming. She could see the gleam in his eye from here.

'Come on, Lara. I don't bite. You've lived under the same roof as me for the last two weeks. You know that.'

'But we haven't been in the same bed.' The words were out before she could stop them as the heat flushed into her cheeks.

He starfished across the bed. 'But look how big it is.'

His T-shirt had crept up a little, revealing the dark hairs leading down to...

He turned on his side again as she gulped. 'Look, this bed is enormous. If you find me that irresistible you can put some pillows down the middle to stop you from sneaking over to my side.' He demonstrated by moving some of the pillows from behind his head into the middle of the bed. The ratfink. He was enjoying every second of this.

'What do you wear in bed?' she blurted out.

'Nothing.' It was a rapid-fire answer complete with wicked gleam.

The heat from her cheeks was starting to spread down the rest of her body. Soon she'd light up the room like a glow-worm. 'You can't wear nothing!'

He grinned and put his arms behind his head again. 'What do you want me to wear?'

'Something. Anything.'

He moved off the bed and walked over to her, grabbing her arm, pulling her away from the doorway and letting the door slam behind her. The room instantly shrank in size. The suite didn't feel so extra-large any more.

Now her nostrils were full of his scents—aftershave, soap and the biggest whiff of pheromones possible. Her vision was completely taken up by his chest and shoulders. And he hadn't let go of her hand. 'I'm sure when it comes to bedtime,' he said huskily, 'I'll find something entirely appropriate to wear.'

She could almost feel his voice skitter over her skin. That Irish accent was so sexy, so enchanting that one tiny Amazonian part of her wanted to drag him back to the bed right now, throw him down and just leap on board.

She wasn't normally as uptight around other people as she was around Reuben.

She sucked in a breath and looked up at him. Those dark brown eyes were fixed on her face. The intensity was shocking. Thank goodness for the little twinkle that was still there.

'You'd better,' she said firmly, 'or this is going to be a long two weeks for you on a hard floor.'

The edges of his lips turned upwards. His breath touched her skin. 'Whatever you say, Lara.'

She nudged her shoulder into his chest and pushed past him. 'Let's get changed,' she said quickly. 'There's a whole world out there and I don't want to miss a second of it.'

And just like that she'd agreed to share her bed with a man she'd only known for two weeks.

CHAPTER SEVEN

THE SHIP GLIDED along the Grand Canal. It was one of the final cruise ships allowed along the Grand Canal before plans changed and they all had to moor outside the canal.

Reuben hadn't expected any of this. Everything about this had been last minute for him and, to be honest, he'd been treating it all like a bit of a joke.

Yes. He needed a holiday. After four years with none at all he deserved one.

More importantly he needed some time away from his current business dealings before his partial eruptions turned into a full-blown Vesuvius version.

Lara's face in the cabin had been a picture. He hadn't even given any thought at all to the sleeping arrangements but it seemed she had and her plans had gone awry.

It was clear she didn't realise just how cute and sexy she looked with that wrinkled nose and wide eyes.

So the wonder of Lara, coupled with the wonder of Venice, was doing strange things to him.

The thought of a short fling with Lara was growing more appealing by the second.

They stood on one side of the ship as they passed the Piazza San Marco, the Doge's Palace and the campanile of San Giorgio Maggiore. The multicoloured buildings, some old and tired with peeling plasterwork, others still proud and pristine with arched windows, balconies and overflowing window boxes, kept them enthralled. There was something about Venice that couldn't actually be captured in a photo or in a travel book. You had to actually *be* there to experience the colours, the sights, the noise.

It seemed that every holidaymaker on the cruise ship was standing on deck to watch their passage out to sea. The sun was beating down on them and after a few minutes Lara gave a little sigh and leaned against him, taking a sip of her cocktail. 'This is just how I imagined it would be.' Her voice sounded sad and without even thinking about it his hand slid around her waist and anchored her to him.

'It's gorgeous,' he said quietly. 'I never even gave this much thought. I knew that Venice was a group of islands but I didn't realise quite how many. Or how different they all are.'

The ship had moved on, passing the island where Murano glass was made and moving past one with that was used mainly as a cemetery. He turned his head a little to face Lara. There was a tear gently rolling down her cheek.

'Hey.' Reuben caught her shoulders and turned her to face him. 'What's wrong? Isn't this the trip of a lifetime? The one you always dreamed of?'

Was this because of him? His teasing earlier about the sleeping arrangements? Lara had always seemed able to play him at his own game, but maybe he'd just stepped too far.

She gave a little nod of her head. 'It is. I know it is. It's just…different from what I expected.'

'How?' Now he could feel his insides curling up.

She gave the tiniest shake of her head and sighed, wiping away another tear. 'I expected to be really excited to be here. To love every minute. But the last few weeks and all the trouble with Josh have just…taken the gloss off things for me. I spent so much time thinking about where we would be going, what we would see.'

She gave the wryest smile he'd seen. 'Now I'm standing here, watching Venice glide past, I'm just realising I've been dumped in the most horrible way. He wasn't even sorry. He didn't really care that I'd caught them. Then to throw away all my things, knowing how that would upset me, and that I wouldn't be able to replace them.' She gave her head a little shake.

'I know it's silly to get upset over an old book.' She pressed her hand against her heart. 'But it meant something to me. I guess things have just hit me all at once. I've been treated like I'm not good enough by a man who is lower than the belly of snake. It doesn't really say that much for me, does it?'

There was an instant burn inside him. He recognised it well. Rage. Fury. The kind of feelings usually channelled into his business dealings. It helped when dealing with some of the volatile sports stars. Not the kind of rage he used in everyday life.

Not since that night with Caleb.

'Garbage.' He grabbed her hand and pulled her towards a set of steps, ushering her up towards one of the exclusive bars.

'Where are we going?'

He pointed to one of the bar stools that gave a view out of the full-length glass windows and gestured to the barman, pointing to a bottle of pink champagne.

The barman didn't hesitate. He produced two champagne glasses, an ice bucket and popped the cork quickly.

Reuben took the champagne and poured it into glasses, the froth and bubbles almost spilling over the edges of the glasses. 'Here.' He handed her one.

'What are we doing?' Her brow was furrowed.

'We're toasting the end of a bad relationship. We're celebrating the fact that Josh didn't manage to ruin your dream. We're saying goodbye to feeling like rubbish and raising our glasses to a new future and a new adventure. No negative thoughts allowed. From here on, it's fun, fun, fun.'

He clinked his glass against hers. He wasn't usually so gung-ho. So nice really. But there it was again. That weird thing about being around Lara and her sad face doing strange things to his insides. He seemed to have a low threshold for her being down.

When he'd first met her two weeks ago she'd been fiery—and still quite angry. And even though she still joked with him it was almost as if uncertainty was taking her over. She'd obviously had too much time to think about all this—too much time to let her confidence falter.

He looked around. In his opinion Lara Callaway was the best-looking woman around here. And apart from being funny, she was quirky and she had a good heart. She had passion. She said she loved looking after Tristan and after a few false starts in life obviously thrived in the job she was currently doing. Maybe if she'd been working the last two weeks she might have been too distracted to get down. Now he was feeling guilty for not being around much, contract negotiations and temperamental clients having filled up most of his days and evenings in London.

But the next two weeks would be entirely different. The next two weeks he'd be around her morning, noon and night. And where might that lead?

Maybe Lara would consider a fling? Some fun on the cruise? Because that's all it could be. He wouldn't be able to offer the Caleb and Addison lifestyle. The happy-ever-after and for ever. He wasn't that kind of guy. He didn't come from that kind of family. But two weeks to try and build a beautiful girl's self-confidence? He could do that.

He shifted on his bar stool. That single thought had sent an imaginary cool breeze over his skin and blood rushing to places it shouldn't. Strange how these things sneaked up on you.

Lara gave him a smile that almost made him sigh with relief. She clinked her glass against his. 'You're right. I know you're right. This year is the end of all ratbag boy-friends. And the start of something new entirely.' She tipped back her head to swallow some of the champagne.

He gulped. Her scent was drifting around him—the same scent she'd worn that day he'd kissed her in the café. And right now he had a prime view of that soft skin at the bottom of her neck…

What was wrong with him?

Reuben Tyler didn't take time to fantasise about women. Normally, he didn't *have* the time. Plus the fact he usually just acted on instinct. He could spot a flirta-tious glance from a million miles away. All he usually had to do was decide whether to go with the flow or not. But Lara was entirely different.

Sure, there was buzz between them. Sure, her lips tasted like no others.

But most of all he'd actually got to know her a little. He knew what kind of coffee she liked. What kind of cake. He knew the type of wine she liked to drink and what kind of takeout food she enjoyed best. All of these superfluous things usually just passed him by. But living under the same roof as Lara for the last two weeks had kind of imprinted them on his brain in a way he couldn't really understand.

She reached over and touched his hand. 'This is great, thanks. Do you want to go and sit back outside? We could look at the information they gave us and decide what trips we want to do at the different ports.'

There was that innocence to her voice. A purity that he'd really never encountered before. Most of the women he met were players. They knew exactly what they wanted and when they wanted it. Lara didn't even have a sniff of that around her. It was refreshing. It was different. And it was clear that he'd been moving in the wrong circles for far too long.

He resisted the urge to say the words hovering on the edge of his tongue. *We'll go wherever you want.*

Maybe it was the nature of holidays that played havoc with the senses. Maybe it was the freedom that he was going to be able to ignore his emails and phone for two weeks.

Or maybe it was the Lara effect.

It made him wary. Was a two-week fling really what Lara would want?

Would that really help rebuild her confidence?

He gave his head a shake. Whatever it was, he had two weeks to figure it out. He refilled the glasses. 'Sure, why not? Let's watch the rest of the Venice lagoon go by.'

His hand went naturally to the small of her back as they headed to the door and he resisted the temptation to let it slide further down.

This could be a long two weeks.

CHAPTER EIGHT

'Do you want to hit the casino?'

'What?' She was sitting on the balcony, reading a book and letting the sun warm her shoulders.

Reuben didn't do relaxation well. He'd been pacing around the cabin for the last hour. He'd already gone for a couple of walks around the ship and flicked through the various channels on the ship's TV.

'Do you want to go to the casino? Put on one of those fancy dresses we bought and let's live a little.'

She lifted her feet down from the table they were resting on and leaned forward, watching Reuben as he paced the room, trying to use up some of his nervous energy. What on earth was wrong with him?

'I've never been to a casino before. What do you actually do in them?'

He looked stunned. 'You've never been to a casino before?'

She shook her head and shrugged her shoulders. 'The only casinos I've seen are the ones James Bond is usually in.'

Reuben walked out and grabbed her hand. 'Well, the casino on board might be quite small, but it's a perfect start. Come and get changed.'

She let him pull her to her feet.

'It'll be the perfect start for the mother of all casinos, the one in Monte Carlo.'

Her eyes widened. 'We can't possibly go there.'

'Why not? We're mooring at Monte Carlo overnight. There's no curfew on the ship. We can be out as long as we like.'

She wasn't sure if he was conscious of his movements but as he said the words he stepped closer to her. Other people might be intimidated by a guy moving into their personal space but things were getting odd with Reuben.

They weren't in a relationship. They weren't actually anything to each other. But from that first stormy meeting every day just seemed to step up a little notch. There was almost expectation now. That waiting...for something. She wasn't quite sure what.

But every time Reuben took a step into her personal space those expectations rose. The electric buzz had been rising slowly, first to a simmer then to some definite bubbles. Everything was just beneath the surface. All it would take was one move, one look, one connection to make everything erupt.

She just wasn't sure she was ready for it.

She'd just broken up with Josh. She should be distraught. She should be giving herself some time to heal and collect her thoughts.

But everything about her was jittery. Her stomach was permanently clenched. Reuben hadn't offered anything. Hadn't mentioned anything. He was here with her now after inviting himself on her holiday.

He was sharing her cabin—sharing her bed with no discussion of what on earth was going on between them. And she couldn't ask. Because then she would be admitting there *was* something.

It was official. Reuben Tyler was the most exasperating man she'd ever met.

She looked up at the brown eyes that were fixed on hers. What would he do right now if she stood up on tiptoe, wrapped her arms around his neck and kissed him—just like he'd kissed her in the store in London?

Maybe it was time she kept him on his toes too?

But right now she couldn't. She gave a tiny shake of her head and a little smile. 'Monte Carlo it is. I can hardly wait.'

Holidays seemed to do strange things to Reuben. He was talking to complete and utter strangers at dinner every night and actually finding their company enjoyable. He was having conversations about things other than sport and stocks and shares.

Every time someone assumed that Lara was his partner he couldn't find the words to correct them. And that was definitely a first for him. He actually liked it that people assumed they were together. He'd nearly blown a quiet gasket when he'd seen some guy leer at her at the bar. But Lara was no shrinking violet. She'd accidentally-on-purpose dropped her iced drink in his lap and promptly left.

Now he was drumming his fingers on the sumptuous piano bar, waiting for Lara to appear before their visit to Monte Carlo's casino tonight. They'd only arrived in port an hour ago and he'd quickly dressed and left her to get ready. He'd been able to tell she was nervous.

Funny thing was he was a little nervous too.

The man next to him made a little strangled noise, choking on his rich Merlot. Reuben spun around to follow his gaze and almost choked himself. Lara was wearing the gold dress, the one that looked completely sheer and was covered with jewels and gold sequins. It gave the illusion of nakedness where there was really none. Just as well he actually knew that—the rest of the men in the bar would continue to keep their eyes entirely on her.

But Reuben couldn't have dragged his eyes away if he'd tried.

Lara's skin had only the tiniest hint of colour, her long blonde hair resting in gently cascading curls down her shoulders. Her only jewellery was a thin gold locket around her neck and her long bare legs finished with her jewelled wedges drew almost as much attention as the dress itself.

She was every inch the belle of the Monte Carlo ball.

His feet moved automatically to meet her. It was almost self-preservation. If he wasn't by her side in an instant some other guy would be. Without even thinking, he slipped an arm around her waist and gave her a kiss on the cheek. 'You look amazing, Lara.'

There was still a glimmer of uncertainty in her face, the tiniest part of her still lacking in self-confidence. He couldn't for a second understand why—and he'd bet every person in the room wouldn't understand either.

But this was Lara. They didn't know her like he did.

She gave a little nod of her head and sucked in a breath. 'Thank you,' she said, running her eyes up and down his formal suit.

This time it was his turn to suck in his breath, even though he didn't understand why. He pointed towards the bar. 'Do you want to have a drink before we go?'

She shook her head. 'No.' Her gaze meshed with his. 'I'd rather just get this night started.'

The words sent a buzz through his entire body. If any other woman had said those words he would immediately have assumed something. Something intimate. But with Lara? He just wasn't sure.

He held out his elbow towards her. 'Then Monte Carlo here we come.'

She slid her arm into his. 'I can't wait.'

* * *

The journey from the ship to the edge of Monte Carlo took only a few minutes. The ship was moored directly underneath the race track and casino.

There were guards standing at the entrance to the world-famous casino and her stomach gave a little flip-flop as they started up the steps. Trouble was she didn't know if the flip-flop was for the venue or the handsome man on her arm.

She hadn't bothered with a jacket but the night air was warm and the lamplight in the street made the jewels and sequins on her dress send scattered lights all around them. She was like her own little kaleidoscope. The kind she'd pressed to her eye as a child. It made her heart flutter in strange little ways. It was like being the star in your own fairy tale.

Reuben's hand was securely placed at the bottom of her spine and from the second they'd stepped off the ship things had seemed different. As if something had just stepped up a notch.

They entered the Salon Renaissance and had their IDs checked quickly. 'I can't believe people from Monaco can't gamble here,' she whispered.

'Neither can I,' he replied in a low voice. 'But the law was made over a hundred years ago. They didn't want to corrupt their own citizens but they're happy to take money from any visitors.' He glanced around as a famous racing driver entered the casino. 'And remember the foreign nationals who reside in Monaco can come here.'

'So I see,' she replied, as she watched the racing driver and his model girlfriend, dressed in a slinky red dress, nod to the doorman and walk in like old friends.

The Salon Renaissance was sumptuous. Everything about the place spoke of opulence and money. There was a variety of gaming rooms all around them. Lara had no clue what was going on in any one of them.

Reuben gave a smile of amusement at the look on her face. 'How about we go and get a cocktail first? Then I'll get us some chips and we can look through the gaming rooms and decide what you want to play.'

'I'm not sure about this,' she murmured, starting to feel a little panicked. Someone like her could easily lose their entire year's income on the turn of a hand of cards. She was completely out of her depth here.

They walked through to the bar. Like everything else it was elegant and immaculate. Lara poised herself on one of the bar stools. The biggest surprise was how busy the casino was. It was still early evening, but everywhere she looked she could see well-dressed people laughing and chatting as if visiting the casino was an everyday occurrence.

She shifted on her stool. The little jewels and sequins on her dress caught the lights from the chandelier above the bar. Thank goodness for the gold dress. Even if she had retrieved her original wardrobe she would never have had anything suitable to wear in here.

Reuben handed her the cocktail list. It didn't even have prices listed and for once she decided not to ask. She scanned the list quickly. 'I'll have a mango daiquiri,' she said with a smile. 'I'd usually have strawberry, but it might be time to try something new.'

She lifted her gaze to meet his just as the breath was sucked out of her body as she realised how that might sound.

Nothing was lost on Reuben—he just had a way of act-ing *way* much cooler than she did. There was the tiniest flicker in his eyes. Then a little quirk as the corner of his lips turned upwards. His beer was much more straightforward, but once they had their drinks he raised his glass to hers. 'To trying something new.'

Her hand trembled. The flirtation was definitely increasing, along the heat between them. Right now they could probably heat up the whole building on their own. She took a sip of the frozen daiquiri and tried not to groan with pleasure at the sharp and sweet cold sensation.

He held his hand towards her. 'Want to have a look around?'

She nodded. There were doors to different rooms all around them. 'Do you know where to go?'

He smiled and pointed with one hand. 'The Hall of the Americas has blackjack, craps, American roulette and baccarat. The White Hall has slot machines. The Salon Europe has English and European roulette, stud poker and thirty forty.'

He might as well have been talking a foreign language. A vaguely familiar-looking woman walked past, glittering with diamonds, her face completely wrinkle-free. Hadn't she won an acting award a few years ago? It was like being the new girl in school all over again. She didn't have a clue where to go or who to talk to. Reuben was the only familiar factor in this whole scenario. She turned to face him. 'Does anywhere play snap or gin rummy?'

He turned to face her, his hand automatically going to her hip. It made her feel a tiny bit more secure. Maybe he would find her lack of knowledge exasperating. Maybe he would get fed up with her and want to go and spend some time at the tables on his own. Her stomach was currently clenching as she watched him.

His fingers moved at her hip, pulling her just a few inches closer. She could almost see something flash in his eyes but it wasn't the usual amusement or tease. This was something different. Almost a form of endearment. 'You don't know how to play any of these games?'

She shook her head and blonde curls cascaded forward over her shoulders. 'No. But I'm sure I could kiss your dice for luck.'

Her whole body was tingling right now. Maybe she was reading this all wrong. Let's face it—she'd hardly been astute when it came to Josh.

But this situation and this *man* felt like a million miles away from her last. Reuben reached up and brushed his finger next to her cheek. Any second now she might actually see stars.

This time she moved. She stepped forward, letting the aroma of him drift through her senses. He leaned forward.

She could smell his shaving gel, the one he'd used as he'd got ready. For some reason she was holding her breath, caught in the gaze of his dark brown eyes. His sexy smile seemed entirely for her only. 'I think you're right.' His voice was low and husky. 'I think you might be my good-luck charm.'

The effect was instant. Butterfly wings against her skin, beating in tiny frantic movements. All parts of her skin. Even parts that were apparently covered.

This couldn't be happening. This just wasn't right.

The hand holding her cocktail glass trembled, even though she tried to steady it.

He was still only inches from her. She could see tiny lines around the corners of his eyes, the hint of shadow around his jaw line and a pair of lips just asking to be kissed.

Her fingers tightened around the stem of her glass. Everything about this was, oh, so wrong. She shouldn't even be thinking like this. Shouldn't even let these thoughts enter her head.

But from the second they'd arrived it was almost as if a fanfare was erupting all around them. Back home in England there had been several moments, several flashes that might have made her think about Reuben Tyler a little differently.

But once he'd kissed her, once he'd made her lips sting and toes curl it had been like a tiny seed in her brain that just unfurled into a giant chestnut tree. With acres of room to swing on. *Stop it!*

She swallowed nervously. It didn't matter she'd already drunk half her cocktail. Her lips were bone dry. Especially when he was staring at them.

Her automatic response was to lick them. But Reuben's gaze didn't move. Normally she would have felt uncomfortable, felt as though she were under the microscope. But everything about this—the grandeur of the surroundings, the volume of people around them, the feel of the expensive dress against her skin, and the way his cologne was weaving its way around her—made her feel a little bold. It was like starring in her own private movie.

She licked her lips again and watched as he straightened his shoulders a little. She matched his move, pressing lightly towards him and letting her breasts almost touch the lapel of his jacket. She bit her lip and kept watch on his dark eyes.

It was the first time she'd ever overtly flirted with a man. Lara was used to speaking her mind, but she wasn't a girl of action, and she'd never been a tease.

Maybe she was having an allergic reaction to the mangoes in the daiquiri? They weren't exactly her normal fruit of choice. It could be that they'd had some strange effect on her body and lowered her inhibitions. Or maybe it was just the giant rush of pheromones emanating from them both and exploding somewhere in the middle.

Whatever it was, the sparkle coming off her dress didn't even begin to capture what was happening between them.

Reuben shifted on his feet, a little uncomfortable. Was

he adjusting himself? She couldn't help the smile that reached from ear to ear.

'Come on,' he said briskly, covering her free hand with his own. 'Let's teach you how to play European roulette.'

He crossed the Salon Renaissance in such long strides she almost had to run to catch up. Now she had pulses shooting up her arm too.

He stopped abruptly and turned to face her, not dropping her hand. 'Did you want to eat first? There are restaurants here.'

She shook her head. Eating was absolutely the last thing she wanted to do right now. Her stomach wouldn't be able to keep a single thing down.

Reuben walked smartly to a booth and changed some money for chips. He turned and handed them to her. She frowned and stared at the multicoloured pile in her hands. 'How much are these worth?'

He paused, as if he was hesitating to tell her. 'They're in euros. The value is on them. It ranges from twenty-five euros to one hundred, five hundred and a thousand.'

'A thousand euros? Are you mad?' She could see heads turn at her rising voice. But she didn't care. She started riffling through the chips. 'Which ones are those? I don't want those. I don't really want the five hundreds either. Even the hundreds make me feel a bit faint.'

'Relax.' He closed both hands over hers, his voice as smooth as silk. 'What can go wrong? You're my lucky charm.'

He slid an arm around her waist and directed her to one of the rooms where they were playing roulette. She watched for a few minutes, her eyes wide. She didn't have a clue what was going on and everyone else looked like they'd been doing this for years.

'I thought we were doing the one where all I had to do was kiss the dice?' she murmured.

He raised his eyebrows. 'Craps? It's complicated. That's in the other hall. I thought I'd introduce you to something a little easier.'

He gave a nod to the croupier and gestured for Lara to sit on a stool.

Lara was so out of her comfort zone that she had no idea she was by far the most stunning woman in the room. She'd started to line up the chips into little coloured piles. It seemed to keep her focused.

Reuben had his arm around her, the length of his body up against her back. Her orange-flowered scent was snaking its way up his nostrils. On anyone else he would hardly notice. On Lara it was tantalising, evocative.

He could see the glances from the other people around the table. They were curious about the new players.

Lara leaned back against his chest and turned her head to whisper to him, 'What on earth do we do now?'

He reached up his hand and pulled her silky soft curls back from her ear to reply. He couldn't help it, his reaction was automatic, but his finger trailed down the soft skin behind her ear and down to the nape of her neck. She twitched against him and he resisted the temptation to do it again. He'd already had one waking up of his anatomy tonight and it seemed like any second there would be another.

He took a deep breath and spoke in her ear in a low voice, his lips brushing against her earlobe.

'You can do lots of different things. The most straightforward way is to bet on red or black. Or you can choose between odd or even numbers. The stakes are lower then. If you want to be a bit more risky you can bet on a column of twelve numbers or a row of three.' His left hand moved to her hip. 'You can put your chip on a line and bet on two numbers—that's a split bet, or you can put a chip on a corner—between four lines.'

She nodded slowly as she studied the table, as if she were trying to take it all in.

He took a final step forward, moving his right hand from the edge of the table and directly onto her thigh. He heard her suck in a breath, but the action just pushed her body further back against his. 'Or you can play things dangerously and only bet on one number. That's the most risky play.'

He let the words hang in the air between them.

They were good at this. Talking innocently about one thing when they were actually implying another. Or maybe it was just he who thought that way? Maybe this was all going completely over Lara's head?

But then she rested back fully against his chest, shifting her hips backwards on the chair and coming into contact with another part of him. She didn't flinch. She didn't move. Instead, she picked up one of the chips, turned it on its edge and rolled it over the back of his hand, which was still firmly on her thigh.

'I'm not quite sure how I want to play,' she said cheekily.

A waiter came past and nodded at their near-empty drinks. 'Same again?' he asked.

Lara shook her head. 'I'll have a lavender fizz.'

Reuben smiled and turned towards her, his lips almost coming into contact with her cheek.

'What on earth's that?'

She smiled. 'Champagne, lavender syrup and raspberry purée.'

He raised his eyebrows. 'You memorised the whole cocktail menu?'

She shook her head. 'No,' she answered innocently. 'Just the ones I liked the look of.'

Reuben nodded to the waiter. 'I'll have the same again and the lady will have a lavender fizz.'

His fingers slid a little further up her thigh. *Her bare thigh.*

He'd seen plenty of glimpses of her thighs in the last few days but he hadn't actually felt how silky smooth they were until right now. If he wasn't careful the roulette table was going to start blurring in front of him.

Lara stood up quickly, leaning across the table and putting her chip down on the number seventeen. He could see the gentlemen on either side of him glimpse the rapidly rising short dress and he moved to block their view.

She gave him a playful smile. 'I think I've decided to take the biggest risk.'

That was it. The blood was roaring in his ears. The palms of his hands were tingling. This was ridiculous. He was in the finest casino in the world and was supposed to be showing Lara around. Instead, he felt like a teenage boy with hormones erupting all over the place.

This was *so* not him. What was different here?

The croupier gave a nod. 'All bets placed?' he said, as he looked around the table.

Ten seconds later his white-gloved hand spun the roulette wheel and sent the ball spinning in the other direction.

Lara was still standing but she backed up against him. 'My first-ever bet,' she whispered.

He was surprised. 'What? You don't even bet on the Grand National?'

She shrugged. 'I don't know a thing about horse racing and wouldn't have a clue how to put on a bet. I've never been in a betting shop in my life. My parents didn't bother with things like that. I used to just pick my favourite jockey outfit from the newspaper and shout for that horse.'

He liked her. He liked her more and more. And it was beginning to creep around him like a big coiling snake. He'd never really felt that connected to any woman before. And he'd never believed in love at first sight. In his world, that was for fools.

It was ironic really but from that first impact—that first blow on the head and that murky blackness as he'd come round and got his first look at Lara, the giant pink teddy bear, something weird had happened to him. He couldn't put his finger on it. He couldn't describe it. Because he didn't really know what it was.

He just knew that he didn't like to see her sad. He'd probably do or tell her anything to help her blink back her tears. And he would have been more than happy to knock her ex into next week. It had taken all his self-control not to.

And here in the casino, he could see her attracting attention. But what struck him most was that Lara hadn't noticed. Her attention was focused entirely on him. And that gave him the biggest buzz in the world.

This place was probably full of billionaires—but that hadn't even crossed Lara's mind. She wasn't calculating. She wasn't a player. He'd spent the last few years mixing in the wrong circles. Lara was like a breath of fresh air.

She sounded as if she might have been a little flighty in the past but it was clear she loved her job and wanted to do the best she could for Tristan. It was refreshing to find a woman who wanted to pay her own way and take care of herself. And it was more than a little infuriating to know she'd been subsidising and taken advantage of by another man.

The wheel was spinning round and round and his hand slipped around her waist and rested on her stomach. He smiled. She was holding her breath, waiting for the ball to rest in one of the numbers on the roulette wheel. Her fingers were clenched into tight fists.

Watching the ball spin round the roulette wheel was almost mesmerising. He could see how people could become addicted to the game but the only thing he was addicted to right now was the look on Lara's face.

The wheel started to slow, the ball moving more slowly almost tripping past the numbers. 'Come on!' she urged.

Her stomach muscles were clenched under his palm. The ball tripped alongside the last few numbers, moving steadily past twenty-five, then seventeen, then thirty-four, before finally coming to rest on number six.

'Oh, no.' Lara sagged back against him and without even thinking he tightened his grip a little. She spun around in his arms, their noses practically touching. It seemed almost natural that her arms lifted and rested on his shoulders. 'Rats,' she said. 'My first bet was a complete doozy. Maybe I should just give up on all this?'

The waiter appeared back with their drinks and set them down on the table next to them. Reuben was conscious of the eyes of people around them watching. They must look like a couple. It was an intimate pose. It spoke of complete and utter knowledge of the other person. And right now he wished that was true.

'Let's finish these drinks.' He smiled. 'We can place a few more bets and then just people-watch if you want.'

She glanced to the side as a well-known movie actor walked past with his entourage. She tilted her head to the side. 'Well, I guess if we want to people-watch, this is the place to do it.'

She picked up her lavender fizz and took a sip. She gave a little hiccup as the bubbles caught in her throat. 'Wow.' She laughed. 'It's delicious.'

He moved forward, this time with him sitting on the stool at the roulette table and positioning her perched against his thigh. It was the oddest feeling but he wanted everyone around—with their admiring glances—to realise that Lara Callaway was with him. *Just him.*

Lara seemed to rest comfortably there, sipping her cocktail as she watched him place a few bets. The casino was getting busier, the tables more crowded, and the Mediterranean heat was rising.

He brushed his hand against her leg again. 'Let's say you try again? One more time—for luck. Betting in the casino at Monte Carlo is something you can tell your kids about.'

Her gaze faltered and dropped down to his hands then slowly up to his face. He wondered what she was about to say and it made his gut twist a little. But after a few seconds Lara smiled and laughed. 'Or when I'm old and grey and in my rocking chair on the porch I can tell my grandkids about this man who hijacked my cruise and introduced me to the high life.'

Something inside him plummeted. Was that really how he wanted to be remembered? As the man who'd hijacked her cruise? It wasn't exactly complimentary. It certainly didn't have any emotion attached to it. He could be anyone—anyone at all. And that's what bothered him most.

It was almost like putting up an automatic shield around himself. 'Introduced you to the high life, eh? Was that what you wanted?' The words didn't seem to come out quite right.

She shook her head. Her hands were still on both of his shoulders and his hands lifted and settled on her hips. She shifted her head from side to side before locking her blue eyes on his. Her voice was low.

'I think this is definitely how the other half lives. Even in another lifetime I couldn't fit in here if I tried.' Her voice sounded a little melancholy and a rueful smile spread across her face. 'But I don't know that I'd want to.'

She pointed to her drink. 'It's nice for one evening—to feel like another person, with the world at their feet. But I kind of like being grounded in reality, and there's nothing like cleaning the muddy football boots of a five-year-old and sticking plasters on bloody knees for that.'

He couldn't help but smile. Just when he'd thought she might disappoint him—even a little—she brought him back to earth with a bang.

Several other women flitted through his mind—women who would have put the entire stash of chips on one bet without a moment's thought. Lara had only used one. She didn't seem that interested in using any more. She knew the value of money better than he did. It was humbling.

He spun her around. 'Let's try once more before we leave the table.'

She gave a nod and picked up one more chip.

'Wouldn't you like to raise the stakes a little higher?'

She met his gaze again. 'I think the stakes are high enough already, don't you?'

He swallowed. For a woman with a certain vulnerability about her she was much better at this than she should be.

She reached across the table and set her chip on the line between fourteen and seventeen. 'There you go. This time I'll try a split bet. Let's see if I can get lucky tonight.' Her cheeks flushed a little.

He laughed. The innuendo level was going off the scale. He pulled her back against him, letting her make no mistake about what her words were doing to him.

The croupier spun the wheel and set the ball in motion. Lara leaned forward again to watch the spinning wheel. Her dress hitched up a little at the back and he tried his best to avert his eyes but the hormones flooding through his system really didn't want to.

The wheel started to slow and Lara shifted from foot to foot.

Her hands clasped together in front of her chest as the wheel and ball simultaneously slowed. She leaned even further forward, her attention rapt. The ball seemed to tease tantalisingly as it jumped from number to number, easily slipping past seventeen.

As it moved excruciatingly slower Lara couldn't hide her excitement. She started to clap her hands together and shift more rapidly from foot to foot. 'Oh…look, look, it's getting closer.' The ball tripped over one, then twenty, then seemed to dangle between twenty and fourteen before finally falling over into the red fourteen.

'I've won!' Lara's shout echoed around the casino, much to the amusement of some of the turned heads. She flung her arms in the air and spun in Reuben's grasp, wrapping her arms around his neck and planting her lips firmly on his.

For a second he was stunned. He knew it was excitement. He knew it was the thrill. But there wasn't a single cell in his body that didn't ache in response.

She tasted of raspberry—and of champagne. His hands slid from her hips to her bottom as he edged her lips apart.

This was totally different from their first kiss. The first kiss had been instinctual. An act of self-preservation—all on his part, with no real thought or consideration about Lara. Until he'd got one hint of her hidden passion and only scratched what lay beneath the surface.

This time it was pure, unadulterated pleasure.

Right now he was wearing his bad-boy label with pride. A more sedate man might have decided those few drinks were enough to impair Lara's decision-making processes.

But Reuben didn't doubt her decision-making at all. Not right now anyway. She was finally letting the walls and barriers she'd built up around herself tumble down.

Tonight she had an edge of confidence he hadn't seen before.

Deliberately or not, she'd just aligned her hips with his, pressing the length of her body with its warm curves against him. It was hitting all the right spots.

His fingers trailed down the side of her cheek to the base of her neck where her pulse was beating a rapid tune against his fingers.

She tilted her head to the side. He could sense one leg lifting from the floor as she tilted her pelvis towards his. Her lips parted, her tongue brushed along his bottom lip. Tantalising.

A wave of anticipation swept his body, making his stomach clench. All of a sudden the walls of the sumptuous casino were pressing in around them. The tiny hairs at the back of his neck stood on end. It felt as if every eye in the house was on them.

He drew back. Lara's heavy eyelids fluttered open, her eyes dark with desire. Her lips were swollen, still open, and her breathing choppy.

She looked almost stung that he'd pulled his lips from hers.

It seemed he wasn't the only one caught in the wave of anticipation.

He sucked in a steady breath, ignoring the amused eyes around them, and picked up their chips from table. He nodded his head at their fellow players. 'Ladies, gentlemen, if you'll excuse us?'

He didn't wait for their acknowledgement, didn't need to see their knowing glances.

He just grasped Lara's hand firmly in his and crossed the casino floor in swift steps.

She hadn't said a single word and he could hear her footsteps pitter-patter behind him as they crossed the impeccably tiled floor. They burst through the casino doors and back out into the cool evening air.

This time he did stop. The fresh air was just what he needed. His arm slid around her waist.

He expected her just to stand there for a few seconds, to let the air cool her heated skin and dampen the electricity between them.

But it seemed he didn't know Lara as well as he thought.

She stepped directly into his line of vision. Her bright blue eyes were flooded with passion and a steely determination. She placed one hand on his chest, under his jacket, the palm of her hand pressing against his thudding heart. Her other hand rested on his jawline.

It was an intimate gesture. A gesture almost of promise.

'What was that?' There was no vulnerability to her voice. No uncertainty. Lara Callaway wanted an answer to her question.

'I don't know,' he said quickly. Because he didn't. He wasn't used to a woman putting him on the spot and calling him on his actions. Mainly because his actions were always invited and definitely reciprocated. He was always straight with women. Things were never going anywhere—his job and lifestyle dictated that, so he made no pretences.

But everything with Lara had started differently. He hadn't met her in a club or restaurant. They hadn't gone for a few drinks together, knowing exactly where things would end.

It didn't matter that they had a room together. In fact, it was probably the biggest problem of all. The biggest elephant in the room.

For Reuben, going to a hotel room with a woman meant just that. One night, sex, with a quick retreat in the morning.

Here, there was no retreat. Nowhere to hide.

Lara's eyes flashed at him again. She leaned forward. For a second he thought she was going to kiss him. Thought he might have a chance to taste those lips again.

There was a roaring in his ears. A flashback to the other day and the hurt and pain he'd witnessed in her eyes. Lara Callaway wasn't someone to be played with. She wasn't someone to have a casual fling with and dump when they got back to London.

He knew her.

And if this went any further he would be the person causing the hurt in her eyes.

He took a step back, removing himself from the warmth of her skin and smell of her perfume. He gave a shake of his head. 'This isn't right, Lara. Not for you. Not for me. I'm not your kind of guy. I can't give you any kind of promise.'

His body was screaming at him, *Fool! Fool!*

The irony of how he normally acted was killing him. But he just couldn't do this.

He couldn't do this to her.

Something flashed in her eyes and she leaned forward. Her soft skin came into contact with his cheek, her voice low. 'Don't give me that. You and I both know we move in different circles. I'm not your barracuda girl. And I don't need any guy treating me as if I'm not good enough. I'm past that.'

She spun on her impossibly high heels. The gold jewels and fringes on her dress spun out as she turned, catching the lamplight from the casino, refracting and lighting up the street around them like disco balls as she ran down the steps and jumped into the nearest cab.

Reuben's breath had caught somewhere in his throat. He could hear the theme tune of a movie play in his ears.

Every part of him was cringing. He'd handled this so

badly. She didn't realise he was walking away because he actually *felt* something for her.

If anything, he wasn't good enough for her, not the other way around.

He turned his head towards the ship moored beneath them as he kicked his heels.

Maybe the walk back would cool him off?

One thing was for sure. He certainly needed it.

CHAPTER NINE

Lara was more than mad. Reuben Tyler had ruined her night's sleep in the world's most comfortable bed, with a stunning view of Monte Carlo. Selfish git.

He hadn't kissed her since that day in the café, so when she'd kissed him last night in the casino she hadn't expected to have to draw him a diagram of what came next.

The guy was supposed to be a bad boy.

So bad, that he'd pulled away from their kiss and practically frog-marched her out of the casino. What on earth had she done that had been so wrong?

Was it against the law in Monte Carlo to kiss in the casino?

She wasn't even sure where he'd gone last night and that made her even madder. She'd been too tense to sleep. Had Reuben gone back to the casino to find a more 'suitable' woman? She had visions right now of finding a huge pair of scissors and shredding all his clothes and tossing them over the balcony.

Now she was lying in bed wondering what on earth to say when he finally showed up.

She hated feeling like this, hated feeling as if she wasn't good enough. She'd already had one dose of that from Josh and she certainly didn't need it from Reuben.

What made her cringe was the fact that she must have read much more into their kiss than he had. He couldn't possibly know the way it had sent electric pulses racing through her senses. The way it had scrambled every sensible thought in her brain. And the way it had sent her imagination into overdrive.

She hadn't wanted him to stop. She'd had very vivid ideas of what she'd wanted to happen next—but he obviously hadn't.

It was embarrassing. It was humiliating. Maybe this was normal behaviour for Reuben because, let's face it, she didn't really know him that well. Two weeks trapped under the same roof as someone didn't mean that you got to know them. It was clear she'd barely scratched the surface.

He'd mentioned no relationships. He hadn't even talked about his family. Just a few hints about bad blood between him and his parents. There were enough pictures of him online with pretty girls to fill a hundred albums. So this was it for him. Find a girl. Kiss her.

Something twisted inside her gut. There was no way bad-boy Reuben didn't follow through to the next event. So what exactly was wrong with *her*?

She flung the covers back, grabbed some clothes and stomped into the shower. Today's stop was Château d'If. She didn't care one bit what Reuben's plans were. She'd dreamt about this place since she'd first read *The Count of Monte Cristo*. There was no way she was missing this place for any man.

Reuben's face creased into a rueful smile as he opened the door of the suite and heard the bang of the bathroom door.

She was up. The fireworks would start any time.

He'd spent the night in one of Monte Carlo's sumptuous five-star hotels. Surprisingly, the bed had felt strangely empty and cold. It might have been just what he'd needed last night, but this morning he could do with a little heat again. And that little flash of satin nightdress and glimpse of leg might be all it would take.

What was wrong with him? He was a fully functioning man. It was inevitable that women would have instinctual reactions to parts of his anatomy. Normally, when he knew the attraction was mutual he wouldn't hesitate to pursue it.

But with Lara? Things felt entirely different.

He was getting to know her in ways he didn't normally get to know other women.

He'd seen the primal fight for survival when he'd first met her, closely followed by the hurt in her eyes and a glimpse of vulnerability. That's what had done it for him.

That's what had made him want to pound Josh into the nearest wall. That's what had made him want to make sure that he didn't hurt her in a similar way.

He loved her one-liners and quick comebacks. He knew that part of it was self-preservation—that wall that she kept around herself. He just wasn't entirely sure what was stopping him from bursting through it to get exactly what he wanted.

Lara had wanted him last night.

Just like he'd wanted her.

The mood, the atmosphere, the surroundings, the way she'd looked, everything had been perfect. If you could plan the perfect evening, that would have been it.

So why had it ended with him sleeping in an empty hotel room?

Because after he'd kissed her, after his hormones had threatened to sweep him away, she'd called him on it. She'd asked him what this was. And he'd been unable to answer. All he'd been able to do was step back. Step away.

Because Reuben Tyler didn't have a clue.

Everything about this was alien to him. A crazy little

thought was starting to spin around in his head. Was this what things were like when you started to fall for a person?

How could people live like this? How could they function?

One hand didn't know what the other was doing. Should he kiss her? Shouldn't he? How could he walk away from Lara the next morning and carry on as normal? Because that's what he'd normally do. But every instinct in his body, every cell was crying out and telling him that this time he couldn't do that.

Caleb. That's the only person he would talk to about any of this kind of stuff. And Caleb would probably laugh him out of the room, because Reuben would *never* bring up this kind of thing. He just wasn't built this way. Or so he'd thought.

He could remember a few years ago Caleb bursting into his flat to tell him he'd met her. He'd met the one. Addison. The woman who'd seemed to hate every single thing about him. The woman that Lara seemed to hold in high regard.

He hadn't got it. He just hadn't. It wasn't that Addison wasn't beautiful and charming, because she was—or at least she could be if she wanted to. And what had been crystal-clear was the love and devotion in her eyes for Caleb. He had never doubted for a second how Addison felt about his friend.

There was a quiet confidence about Addison that made her different. She'd never scream. She'd never shout. Reuben had experienced a few of Caleb's previous girlfriends. At one point he'd asked him if he shopped in Tantrums-R-Us.

And it didn't matter that Addison didn't really like him. What mattered was what he saw when Caleb and Addison were in a room together. The way their eyes could find each other across a crowded room. The way Caleb would stop in mid-sentence just to catch his wife's eye and send her a smile.

A special kind of smile that made you wonder what it meant.

All of this had been in some silly cosmic cloud above Reuben's head. He'd never got it. But more importantly he'd never *wondered*. And now he did.

He'd certainly never witnessed it at home. His parents could barely stand to be in the same room together. They had been hateful to each other—more obsessed with money and prestige. It hadn't been an environment to bring a child up in. He could testify to that.

But Reuben always knew how to play a deal. Years of being a sports agent had made him able to read people and know how to deal with them.

Now, for the first time, he'd no idea what to do next.

And it unnerved him. Lara Callaway unnerved him.

He'd thought that nigh on impossible.

She was ready. She was ready to face the world and come out fighting. Bree had a good eye. The white Capri pants and pink printed shirt covered in flying birds was knotted at her waist. She pulled her blonde hair into a ponytail and finished with a slick of pink lipstick. All she needed now was her wedges.

She flung open the bathroom door and stepped straight into Reuben's broad chest. This suite wasn't really as big as it needed to be.

'Owf!'

He held up his hand. Her wedges were dangling from his finger. 'Thought you might need these.'

She stared up at his face. He was smiling. There was no trace of last night. He'd changed into a short-sleeved shirt and trousers. It was clear he was ready to go to Châ-teau d'If. Where on earth had he been?

She sniffed unconsciously—trying to find the smell of another woman on him. But there was nothing. All she got was a huge whiff of Reuben Tyler's pheromones. The thing that drove her nigh on crazy.

'Have a good night?' she snapped.

It was stupid. Even though she was still mad with him, he was here. Here, with her.

He gave a nonchalant nod. Or he tried to. She could see the glimmer of worry behind his eyes. 'I checked into a hotel in Monte Carlo. Didn't want to upset you any more.'

Her stomach flipped over and unwanted tears brimmed behind her eyes. That made him sound considerate. As if he'd actually thought about what had happened between them last night. As if she wasn't quite as unworthy as last night had made her feel.

It still didn't help the fact that he looked relaxed and refreshed after sleeping in a comfortable hotel last night while she'd tossed and turned all night.

'The tour doesn't leave for another hour. We've plenty time for breakfast. Let's go to the restaurant this morn-ing. The buffet is always a bit frantic.'

He was talking as if nothing had happened. But, then, to Reuben, obviously nothing had happened. She didn't know whether to react or not.

He leaned against the wardrobe and folded his arms across his chest. 'You know, some people might ask ques-tions about why you want a visit a prison on an island so much?'

How should she play this? She could hit with all her emotions from last night. But in the cool light of day they seemed a bit out of place. A bit over-dramatic. Maybe she should do what he was doing? Act as if nothing had happened.

She picked up her bag. 'Some people might find that's none of their business,' she answered smartly, as she grabbed her wedges and pushed her feet into them.

She headed for the door, pretending not to notice that Reuben was following her. It was obvious he fully intended to accompany her as usual this morning. Confusion was fluttering through her mind. Didn't he even want to talk about last night? Want to talk about that kiss?

They rode up in the central glass elevator and stepped out at the restaurant. Reuben had been right. It was much calmer here. Sometimes the breakfast buffet felt like survival of the fittest. Why hadn't she thought to come to the restaurant before?

A waiter showed them to their table and took their order. 'Toast and poached eggs and lemon tea, please.'

'Toast, bacon, a fried egg and some coffee, please.' Reuben nodded.

The waiter disappeared quickly.

Lara licked her lips. She was determined not to speak first, determined that he not know how much his rejection last night had hurt.

The ship was due to dock at Marseille later this morning. There was a variety of excursions available but Lara had already pre-booked the one to Château d'If. It had been one of the reasons she'd picked this particular cruise.

'What's the attraction with Château d'If?' he asked again.

She picked at the white linen tablecloth. 'I read a lot as a kid. I know that Alexander Dumas used it for inspiration for *The Count of Monte Cristo*. I've always wanted to visit it.'

'You wouldn't rather browse the shops in Marseille?'

She shook her head. 'And look at more things I can't afford? No, thanks. I'd much rather see the island that inspired my favourite book.'

The waiter appeared again with the coffee and lemon tea. Lara poured her tea and took a sip just as Reuben's phone buzzed.

She frowned as he pulled it from his pocket. 'Who needs hand-holding today?'

He glanced at the screen and pushed the phone back into his pocket. 'Nobody.'

She kept her gaze steady. 'Is that the footballer again? Are you still ignoring his calls?'

He sighed. 'And his voice mails and his texts and his emails.'

She smiled. 'He's persistent, then?'

Reuben nodded.

The waiter appeared and placed their breakfasts down before them. Lara started buttering her toast. 'Is that a good or a bad thing?'

This time it was Reuben who frowned. 'I'm not sure. If you'd asked me last week I would have told you that an agent should always be available for his clients.'

She paused her knife. 'And now?'

He met her gaze. 'I don't know. I've answered any queries from all my other clients. But none of them are as demanding as he is. They can all have their moments—but none of those are quite like his.'

'Does he even know he's being unreasonable?'

Reuben shrugged. 'That's the biggest issue. I don't think so. By the time he finally gets me he'll be furious and probably give me an earful.'

She picked up the salt and pepper. 'So why haven't you dumped him?'

He took a sip of his coffee. 'That's exactly what Caleb asked me. He doesn't like him either.'

Lara shook her head. 'Then I don't get it. The guy gives you constant headaches. He's disrespectful to those around him. He treats the people at the club poorly. In fact, he treats most people in life poorly. Why continue to represent someone like that? Surely his behaviour reflects badly on you too?' She paused for a second as she cut her eggs. 'Or is the pay cheque just too much?'

His fork stopped midway to his mouth. 'Why would it be about the money?' he snapped.

She raised her eyebrows. 'Because there doesn't seem to be another single good reason to keep him on your books.'

Reuben shifted in his chair. It was one of the few times she'd actually seen him looking uncomfortable.

He sighed again. 'It's not quite as easy as that.'

She sat down her knife and fork. 'Well, explain it to me.'

Reuben ran his fingers through his hair. 'Not everyone has a fairy-tale life, Lara. I brought him here from Brazil. He might not have come from the slums but he wasn't far off it. He started with one of the lower-league clubs, but as soon as his talent was noticed, the offers came in thick and fast. He wasn't used to having money. He's not used to fame or the way celebrity is here. I feel as if I've left him exposed to something he wasn't ready for.'

She could see the worry etched on his face. 'How long has he been here now?'

'Four years.'

She tried to be reasonable. 'In that case, he's had four years to learn how to deal with things. He's had four years with English clubs. He's had plenty of time to learn some manners and how to conduct himself. If he hasn't learned by now, it's unlikely he will.'

She took a deep breath. He'd made that little comment about fairy-tale lives. It seemed to have opened a door for her.

'Tell me about Ireland,' she said.

'What do you want me to tell you?' His reply was kind of sharp.

'You haven't mentioned much about your family. Do you have brothers, sisters? Do you see a lot of your mum and dad?'

He twitched. Or was it a visible shudder? 'I'm an only child.'

'And do you go back home much?' she pressed.

He almost rolled his eyes. 'Not if I can help it.'

She put down her knife and fork. 'What does that mean? Surely you never got into that much trouble at home?'

He shook his head. 'Even if I had, no one would have noticed. Not everyone has the idyllic parents that you do, Lara.'

She felt offended. 'What's that supposed to mean?'

He shrugged as he kept eating. 'You've said that your mum and dad are great. They'd be happy to have you back home and you'd be happy to go back if you could.' He shook his head. 'Let's just say I'm at the other end of the spectrum.'

She frowned. 'What does that mean?'

'It means my parents couldn't wait to send me to boarding school and I couldn't wait to go.'

Her stomach twisted. This was all so wrong. No kid should feel like that. 'You don't see your parents?'

'Not if I can help it. I went to see Dad four years ago in hospital and that was it. In all my life I can't remember my mother and father being in the same room and not fighting. Most of the time they didn't even realise I was there.'

Lara sucked in a sharp breath. 'That's awful. Why haven't they just divorced?'

He shook his head. 'Strict Catholics. They prefer to make each other—and everyone around them—miserable.' He paused for a second. 'Don't get me wrong—I've always had a roof over my head, clothes on my back, food on the table. Did I ever have anyone ask me how my day was? Give me a hug or a kiss? Not a chance.'

Lara couldn't eat any more. 'That's terrible. I'm sorry, Reuben, no kid should experience life like that.'

He sat down his knife and fork. 'I guess I should appreciate the fact they sent me to school and I met Caleb. His family are great. They were my first real example of what a family should be. Up until that point I thought most people lived like I did. Once I realised the love and attention Caleb had from his mum and dad it made me resentful and angry.' He took a sip of his coffee. 'Now, a few years on, I'm adult enough to realise I don't need toxic people in my life and step away.'

Lara could feel tears in her eyes. She reached across the table and squeezed his hand. 'You told me before that you knew Caleb would give up his life for his wife and his child. And I know you're right. He's a great dad and a great husband.' She smiled. 'He might have a bit of the workaholic in him, like you, but I've never doubted his devotion to his family. I'm glad you had a chance to see that not all parents are like yours.'

There was silence for a few minutes. She didn't feel the need to fill it with endless chatter. She was trying to get her head around what he'd just told her. It was making her see Reuben in a whole new light. Maybe the way he'd been brought up was affecting his ability to make connections in life? Maybe that was why he had trouble letting people in?

Reuben shook his head a little. 'I was jealous, you know.'

Lara looked up. 'What do you mean?'

He sighed. 'Caleb and I always spent a lot of time together. Once he met Addison...' His voice tailed off.

She tilted her head to the side. 'You got dumped?'

She probably didn't mean it quite like that but the notion was close enough.

He gave a hollow laugh. 'It introduced me to the concept of happily-ever-after. I'd never believed in it. I still don't know if I do and Caleb called me on it. That—and a few other things.'

'You fell out?'

She got the distinct impression there was much more to this.

'Not quite.' He shook his head and stood up, holding out his hand towards her.

She hesitated. After last night did she really want to hold hands with him? But something had changed. His bad-boy edges had chipped off a little. He wasn't as full of bravado as he'd originally seemed.

She pushed her chair back, slipped her hand into his and headed towards the shore and the coaches that were lined up ready to take them on their tour.

It was only a short journey along the coast to where the small boats waited to take them across to Château d'If.

As she stepped down from the coach Lara gave a little gasp. 'It's even more perfect than I imagined.'

Reuben looked at her in surprise. 'A prison? Perfect? That's an unusual description.'

He held out his hand again for hers as she took the last few steps down and walked to board the boat. The white limestone island seemed to rise out of the perfect blue sea with the fortress taking up most of the area. 'I know it's supposed to be one mile away but it looks almost close enough to touch,' she said in wonder.

The boat ride only took ten minutes and the water was much choppier than it had originally looked.

They stepped onto the island to be met by a tour guide who showed them around.

'The history of this place is amazing,' Reuben agreed. 'I can't believe that one of the prisoners was here for nearly twenty years.'

'I like how the cells are all so quirky and different,' Lara said, as she walked up the flight of stairs and peered inside one of them, fingering the sign outside where previous prisoners' names were inscribed.

'You do know that the *Man in the Iron Mask* wasn't actually imprisoned here?'

She smiled and moved to stand behind some bars. 'I know that. But I like the legend. It makes the whole place a little more magical.'

They moved outside and stood at edge of the fortress looking back over the Bay of Marseille. Lara leaned against the fortress wall. 'Look how close Marseille looks. I wonder how many people died trying to reach it and getting caught in the currents.'

He was smiling at her again. 'You like to capture the whole moment, don't you?'

She turned back to face him, her hair getting blown around like crazy in the wind. His hand reached up brushed the side of her face. 'Why else come?' she said quietly. 'There isn't much point if you can't try and get into the spirit of things.'

His gaze locked with hers. It hadn't come out quite as she'd meant. She hadn't been talking about last night. She really hadn't. But now she couldn't drag her gaze away from his. The brisk breeze had made all the little hairs on her arms stand on end. He took a step closer to her. 'So, tell me what you really think.'

Her mouth was instantly dry. His body had blocked out some of the wind sweeping around her, stilled her hair and kind of caught the air between them. For a few seconds she couldn't hear the squawking birds around them. The voices of the other tourists were lost. It was just him and her.

She licked her lips. She was determined not to let those brown eyes pull her in. She'd let that happen in the casino the night before—and where had that got her? The wind was rippling his shirt against the muscles of his chest. It was hard not to look. Hard not to let her hand automatically reach up and rest itself there.

She lifted her chin towards him. 'That's one thing you can count on, Reuben. I'll always tell you what I really think.'

He sucked in a breath. She could feel it beneath her palm and his fingers curled at the side of her cheek. He didn't miss a beat. 'And that's why I'm here, Lara.' There was something in the way his Irish accent folded around her name. Held it there for a few seconds. Cherished it even.

The edges of his mouth turned upwards and a glint of gold lightened those dark eyes. It lightened the moment, letting the breath she hadn't realised she was holding escape from her lips.

His hand dropped and rested behind her waist, exerting the tiniest bit of pressure to turn them both towards the view. She relaxed a little, taking in the sweeping sights of Marseille and the multitude of white yachts in the harbour. It really was another life—another world. A whole other bank balance.

She rested her head against his shoulder. 'This place seems as if it should be something else entirely.'

His fingers drummed against her waistband. 'What do you mean?'

'I kind of wonder why some billionaire hasn't swept in here with some ridiculous offer and tried to buy this island. Couldn't you imagine this place with the fortress transformed into some sumptuous private dwelling with a whole host of glass glinting in the sun? It could be like something from a James Bond movie, you know, with lots of glamorous women in floor-length sweeping gowns drinking cocktails with men in tuxedos.' She glanced around. 'I bet this place could even have its own helipad.'

She waved her hand in front of her. 'And all the beautiful people of Marseille would stare over at the island and wonder exactly what was going on here.'

She turned to face Reuben. He gave an almost imperceptible shake of his head and a grin was plastered to his face.

'What?' she asked.

'You,' he said. 'I had no idea you had such a wild imagination.' He reached over and tapped his finger on her forehead. 'What on earth else goes on in there?'

'Wouldn't you like to know?' she quipped, as she started to walk away.

It was impossible to ignore the curvy bottom in the white capri pants sashaying in front of him. Bree, the personal shopper, had been right. The pants and shirt knotted right at her navel made the most of all Lara's assets, hugging her curves in all the right places. As she walked ahead she reached up and caught her blonde hair, tying it back up in a ponytail.

He preferred it down, but she looked good no matter how she wore it.

He could sense the admiring glances around them. Everyone here must think that he and Lara were a couple. And that wouldn't be a surprise—because they seemed to act like it. He wasn't afraid to touch her—just like she wasn't afraid to touch him. She regularly took his hand, put her hands on his arm or chest, or reached out and touched his face.

The strange thing was he was beginning to ache for her touch. It all seemed so natural. It all just seemed to fit. And he was beginning to wonder what things would be like when they got back to reality.

Back in London, he wouldn't spend much time at Caleb's house. The work on his own property should be complete, and Addison didn't exactly roll out the welcome wagon for him. And she certainly wouldn't appreciate him trying to hang around her nanny.

The thought of not being able to see Lara every day didn't sit comfortably with him. But what on earth could he do about it?

He knew that she hadn't been happy last night—she probably thought he'd screwed things up between them. He'd have liked nothing more to have taken her back to the cabin and undressed her—but where would that have left them?

He didn't want to have a fling with Lara. He didn't want to wake up the next day and make some excuse to leave. But talking about relationships and feelings just wasn't his thing. Guys just didn't have those conversations. Or maybe he was just hanging around with the wrong people?

His parents had certainly never encouraged it. They couldn't face up to their own relationship failings so they couldn't possibly offer any advice that he would take notice of. They'd never been that interested in him. And as he'd grown older he'd been wise enough to distance himself from them completely.

Lara had stopped to chat to a couple of elderly ladies who were also on the cruise. One of them threw back her head, laughing, as Lara's cheeks flushed pink.

He walked over and slid his arm around her waist. 'What have I missed?'

The pinkness in her cheeks deepened and she waved her hand as the ladies dissolved into another fit of laughter. 'Oh, nothing, we were just chatting.'

One of them tapped Reuben on the arm. 'And I wonder who we could have been talking about?' she said coyly. She reached over and grabbed Reuben's phone from his hand. 'Here, let me take a picture of you two lovebirds. You make such a gorgeous couple.'

They barely had time to pose before she handed the phone back and the two ladies walked away, still laughing.

Reuben turned to face her, his fingertips coming into contact with the sliver of bare skin at her waistline. 'James Bond again?'

She shook her head. 'Unfortunately not.'

'Then what?'

She shook her head again. 'Nothing.'

'Come on, tell, it's half the fun.'

She put her hand over his and started to walk back towards the boat. 'Believe me, my imagination has *nothing* on theirs.'

'Now, that sounds *really* interesting.'

She tapped her finger on his chest and gave him a wink. 'Just as well I don't kiss and tell.'

She walked across the gangplank back on board as he stared down at his phone. Two photos had been taken in rapid succession. One showed them posing and smiling a little awkwardly, and another showed him with his arm around her waist and her hand touching his chest. They were looking at each other with the beautiful backdrop of Marseille behind them. This one had no pose about it. It was entirely natural. Their smiles were genuine and the chemistry reached out to grab him.

He gulped and pushed the phone deep down into his pocket.

There were a million pictures of him with glamorous women on the internet. But one thing was for sure—none of them looked like that.

* * *

Two hours later they were back on the cruise ship, lying next to the pool. Lara had changed into her pink bikini and sarong and was trying her best to read the latest bestseller.

Sunglasses were a godsend. She could hold the book in her lap while she secretly spent the whole time sneaking glances at the guy next to her on the sun lounger.

She'd had a few views of Reuben's bare chest before. His muscles were well defined, there was a definite hint of a tan and a fair sprinkling of dark hairs. But couple that with the dark hairs on his defined calves and she was seeing a whole lot more than she normally did.

She gave a little smile as an Italian guy at the other side of pool dived in wearing barely-there white Speedos.

Reuben groaned and rolled over onto his belly. 'Don't tell me you're watching the guy on parade.'

She leaned forward. 'What if I am?'

'Should I have pulled my Speedos out of my bag? Is that what it takes to get some attention around here?'

She laughed and put her book down. 'All it takes to get some attention around here is the promise of a cocktail over at the bar.'

Reuben stretched his arms above his head. It was so easy when her eyes were hidden to have a quick glance at the dark curling hairs on his abdomen leading in one direction.

He sat back up and reached out his hand. 'Done. A cocktail it is.' He nodded his head towards the pool. 'I can't take the competition here anyway.'

They walked over to the nearby bar and sat down. Lara picked up the menu and started to peruse it as the bartender approached. 'What will it be?' He smiled.

Reuben gave her shoulder a nudge. 'What takes your fancy?'

She shook her head at the obvious innuendo. 'Speedos,' she whispered under her breath.

He groaned and turned to the bartender. 'I'll have a beer.'

The bartender nodded. 'And for the lady?'

She sighed and put the menu down again. 'I'm not sure. What do you recommend? I prefer cocktails with rum.'

He pointed to one on the menu. 'How about this one? The sunset cruiser? It has rum, peach, melon, a dash of lime and some Angostura Bitters.'

She grinned. 'Sounds tempting. Count me in.'

Reuben leaned his arm against the bar and raised his eyebrows at her. 'Are you going to taunt me all day?'

She gave a little nod. 'I think you deserve it.'

The sun was shining brightly above them, warming their backs and making her feel more relaxed. 'You should try and catch me,' she teased. 'I'm probably on the re-bound.'

The bartender placed their drinks down and Reuben picked them up and carried them over to a table shaded by a parasol, his lips set in a firm line.

She sat down in the shade and took a sip of her cock-tail. Gorgeous. It hit the right spot.

Reuben was chewing his lip but his dark eyes were fixed firmly on her.

'What if I don't want you on the rebound?'

'You don't seem to want me at all.'

She could almost feel the temperature around them plummet and it was nothing to do with the shade.

'I guess I'm not good enough.' Her stomach curled as she said the words. 'But I don't really want to be a vacant blonde, hanging on to your arm in a designer dress, like all the others.'

His back straightened and she could see him bristle.

He was mad, but trying to control it. He took a swig of his beer. His jaw tightened. 'I like you,' was all that came out.

'Just not that much,' she said swiftly, as she took another sip.

This wasn't nearly as uncomfortable as it should be. The ship had just set sail again. There really was no escape for either of them. She was confused about last night. Surely she hadn't read things wrong? Their chemistry had practically lit up the whole of Monte Carlo.

And it was kind of amusing to see Reuben Tyler struggle to find words.

A cool breeze swept over her skin. Maybe he was just trying to be kind, when what he really wanted to say was that he just wasn't attracted to her at all. Now, that really *did* make her stomach lurch in all the wrong ways.

She was already feeling exposed—and sitting in her bikini and sarong didn't exactly help. She took another sip of the cocktail, hoping the rum would calm her nerves.

She could see a little tic in Reuben's jaw.

He took another swig of his beer. Did he need Dutch courage too? He sighed and set the bottle down with a clunk. 'I like the fact you're not a vacant blonde.'

She licked her lips. 'Really?'

He shifted in his seat. 'I like being around you.'

It was like getting blood out of a stone. It seemed that when it came to the emotional stuff Reuben was hard work.

'I like being around you too,' she replied.

He wasn't looking at her any more. He'd fixed his eyes on the horizon. 'But it's awkward.'

'Awkward how?' This didn't seem to be going so well.

He ran his fingers through his dark hair. 'I'm not good at relationships.'

'Is that what this is? A relationship? I wasn't sure we'd got that far.' She started playing with the straw in her drink. Nothing like talking about feelings to make you feel like an awkward teenager again.

He lifted his hands up and let out a huge sigh. 'I don't really know how to do this.'

She almost laughed out loud. 'What do you normally do, Reuben? See a girl, ask her out? Date once, and that's it?'

'Usually.'

'Haven't you ever had a proper girlfriend? Lived with someone before? Had someone you would introduce to the family?'

This time he spoke a little more quietly. 'If I introduced anyone to my family they'd have to be wearing a suit of armour.'

She reached over and squeezed his hand. She had such a great relationship with her mum and dad that she couldn't really imagine how it was for him. They'd been having such a wonderful time she didn't want to darken his mood, so she pulled her hand back and lifted her eyebrows. 'My mum's getting desperate for grandkids. I think the next guy I bring back home she'll lasso for me and drag him down to the church!'

Reuben threw back his head and laughed. 'I'd better watch out, then.'

She nodded. 'You'd better. What's your maximum number of dates, then?'

'Honestly? I think it was six.' He shrugged his shoulders. 'And I spent two weeks with you in London, then our time on board, of course.' There was a little sparkle in his dark eyes again. 'You've already beaten the record.' The more he spoke the thicker his accent got. It was doing crazy things to her pulse.

'Even though we've barely kissed?'

He gave a tiny nod of his head. 'You think I didn't want to?'

Her gaze meshed with his. 'Oh, I could *feel* you wanted to.'

He leaned back in his chair and threw up his hands again. 'That's just it. You know I want to. But I like you. I don't want to hurt you. I have no idea where this could go.'

She stirred her drink again. 'And you don't want to find out?'

He folded his arms across his chest. 'You know I do. But you see the kind of job I have, Lara. I'm hardly in the country for any time at all. I spend most of my life in mid-air. How can something work when one of us is never here?' He picked up his beer again and leaned his elbows on the table. 'Anyway, you might have forgotten but you've got a bit of a reputation.'

She jerked back. 'I have?'

He was teasing again. She could tell. Every time he did it, a little glint appeared in his eyes again.

He looked up through heavy lids. This man could be *so* sexy. 'You have. You've got a bit of a reputation for picking losers. I'm worried I'll get labelled.'

She picked up her drink mat and flung it at him. 'I can think of a whole host of other words.'

He laughed. 'Seriously, though, what are you going to do when we get back home?'

She shrugged. 'What else would I do? I'm going to look after Tristan. Caleb and Addison will be back by then and I love my job, he's a great kid.'

A few lines appeared on his forehead. 'Did you always want to be a nanny?'

She shook her head. 'No, I told you. I kind of fell into it.' She counted off on her fingers. 'So far, I've been a nanny, a strawberry picker, worked in a bar, waitressed, spent three dismal months in a call centre, lost someone's messages as a PA and...' she paused and raised her eyebrows '... I even spent two months volunteering at a zoo.'

'What?'

She giggled. 'Believe me, the penguins *stink*!'

He looked serious again. 'So, what was your dream job when you were a kid?'

She sat back for a moment. 'Wow. I think the last person to ask me that my gran.'

'And what did you say?'

A wave of disappointment swept over her. It was odd. It had been a long time since she'd felt like this—as if she hadn't really fulfilled her potential. But the worst part about it was the way she couldn't stop hostile thoughts towards Reuben because he'd asked the question.

She took a few seconds before she finally answered. 'I used to have lots of romantic ideas about working at NASA—even though I couldn't pass physics. Or owning a florist shop or being a TV presenter.'

He gave a little nod. 'Interesting choices.'

'It gets better. I even wanted to be the female version of Indiana Jones and study archaeology.'

He held out his hands. 'Every day's just a surprise with you, isn't it?'

She gave a rueful smile. 'What I really wanted to do was study English at university. I wanted to study English then maybe go on to be a journalist. I got the grades, got the place and then…Gran died. It was as if all my energy and focus disappeared. I couldn't get my head in the right place to study. I decided to take some time off and the rest—as they say—is history.'

'And you'd never consider going back?'

She shook her head. 'I'm twenty-six, Reuben. I'd be the oldest student in the class. They'd call me Grandma.'

He finished his beer and stood up, holding out his hand towards her. 'Then they'd have me to deal with. Come on, let's go and get changed for dinner. We need to plan for Pisa tomorrow.'

She took the last sip of her cocktail and slipped her hand into his. It felt as if it belonged there.

She'd dreamed about coming on this cruise for so long—but her dream had never quite looked like this. Reuben was having a whole host of effects on her she hadn't banked on. And it was clear that the chemistry was still simmering beneath the surface.

Now he had her brain spinning in a whole host of other ways. She wasn't just distracted by the handsome man in front of her—she was also distracted about the things she'd pushed to the back of her brain. Was applying to university again really an option for her? She hadn't even considered it until now. And was this really a time to start thinking about another relationship? She'd just got out of one and was getting her life back on track, having the space and control to make decisions for herself. Did she want anything more? The sun warmed her shoulders as they crossed the deck towards the bar again.

Reuben Tyler was full of surprises. What would come next?

CHAPTER TEN

THE PHONE BUZZED in his pocket again. His footballer client was getting beyond obnoxious. Lara had no idea that he'd actually had three different conversations with the guy since he'd got here—every time telling him to smarten up his act. None of those words seemed to be having an effect.

It was just as well he was in the middle of the Med right now because if he was in the same room as his client he might actually bounce Mr Arrogant into next week.

Any day now the club would cancel his contract because of his antics and Reuben was secretly counting down the days.

Lara was chatting to the two elderly, mischievous women—Doris and Daisy—again. They seemed to be spending most of their time teasing her. All three were currently trying on a whole array of wide-brimmed hats from a street vendor. The Italian sun was positively scorching today.

He walked over swiftly and thrust some bills at the street vendor, paying for all three hats. 'It's on me, ladies,' he said swiftly. 'I don't think I've ever seen anything so ridiculous in my life.'

All three faces turned towards him, laughing. The hats *were* ridiculous. Lara's was pink with a huge yellow flower, Doris and Daisy's bright green and bright blue respectively, both adorned with bright orange flowers.

Doris wagged her finger at him. 'Thank you kindly.

But don't come moaning to me when you've got sunstroke or blisters on the back of your neck.'

They wandered off as Lara put her bag over her shoulder. She was wearing the pale pink dress they'd bought in London and looked as pretty as a picture. The bright pink hat actually suited her. It was quirky. Just like Lara.

His heart stopped. That was it. That tiny little thought had just caused a ricochet around his body.

This was it. This must be exactly how Caleb felt about Addison.

And it had taken until today, watching her laughing in the sunlight, for him to realise exactly how he felt.

He didn't want to wake up next week without Lara in his life. He didn't want to have to skulk around to Caleb's house in order to see her again.

Was this what it was like to be in love?

He couldn't help himself. He wrinkled up his nose and shifted on his feet. It wasn't as if he had an example to follow. His mother and father had spent most of their married life fighting. He'd never seen a single moment between them to make him think they'd ever been in love. And although he'd missed Ireland when he'd been sent to Eton as a teenager, it had actually been a relief to get away from the atmosphere in the house. And once he'd left he'd had no intention of returning on a permanent basis.

So love was a bit of stranger to Reuben. Sure, he'd watched as many corny movies as the next guy—but even they made him feel uncomfortable. He'd loved his grandmother and his grandfather but that kind of deep love and affection was different from the way his heart was beating a rapid tune against his chest now.

That kind of love didn't cause pins and needles down his arms and legs and make him bite his lips to stop them tingling. He took the tiniest step backwards.

He wasn't entirely sure he liked this. He didn't doubt

for a second the kind of person Lara was. She was good. She brought out a whole side of him he hadn't even known was there.

But certain things twisted away at his gut. Things he wouldn't say out loud for fear of offending her. Lara already had some ridiculous idea in her head that she wasn't good enough. The last thing he wanted to do was perpetuate that myth.

But deep down it bothered him that the woman he loved worked for his best friend. It shouldn't matter. He shouldn't care. She'd already told him she was doing a job that she loved.

Was it wrong that he thought she had so much more potential? Was it wrong that he really wanted her to fulfil her dreams?

She was proud. She was independent. He already knew these things. She wanted to pay her own way in life and save hard for the things that she wanted.

He squirmed as he thought about how he hadn't had to consider money in a long time. He was no billionaire. But he was definitely in the category directly below that—in his line of work most agents were. And living in London certainly didn't come cheaply. He hadn't even admitted to her that he actually had more than one property.

The places in the US had become essential since he spent so much time over there—one on the west coast and an apartment on the east coast. Having his own space was so much better than constantly living in hotels. In the next few weeks he would close on a property in Ireland too. He hadn't even viewed it personally—just online. But he knew the area well and it felt good to buy something in Ireland that wouldn't have any ties to his parents and their complicated relationship.

'Reuben, what are you doing?' Lara shouted from the end of the row of street vendors lining the outside of the

Piazza del Miracoli, which held the Baptistery, the Leaning Tower and the cathedral. 'Come on!'

He smiled and hurried after her, reaching the entranceway to the square. The brilliant sunshine was glinting off the white marble of the three buildings. It was dazzling. A real suck-in-your-breath moment. Lara had stopped dead in front of him and he stepped closer putting a hand on each of her hips.

'That was a bit unexpected,' he murmured in her ear. He was talking about the view. Of course he was talking about the view.

He could see the smile painted across her face. It reached from ear to ear. She'd lifted her hands and placed them on her chest. 'Wow,' she breathed. 'Just, wow.'

She leaned back a little against him. It was odd how he was beginning to appreciate the little things. Before he hadn't really gone for any touchy-feely stuff with women. He'd never really had that kind of connection before. But with Lara things felt entirely natural and had done from the beginning. He was relishing it. Liking how much he actually enjoyed it.

'What do you want to do first?'

She eyed the line of cafés across from the three monuments. 'Did the tour guide give you tickets for the tower?'

He nodded and pulled them from his pocket. They had a time stamped on them. Her stomach gave a little growl. 'How about we stop for something to drink first and then work our way around the monuments?' She slid her hand into his as he nodded and headed towards the first café with empty tables out front.

Lara ducked her head in the shop door. 'Nope, not this one.'

He frowned and followed her to the next one. 'What was wrong with that one?'

She stuck her head inside the next one, eyed the glass

cabinet full of cakes and shook her head again. 'Not this one either.'

He looked at the huge array of cakes and pastries and held out his other hand. 'What? Not enough cakes for you?'

She led him to the next doorway, peeked inside and turned around with a wide smile on her face. 'Now, this one will be perfect.'

He glanced inside. It seemed exactly the same as the others. 'What is it?' he whispered. 'What did I miss?'

She pointed with her finger. 'That.'

He followed her finger to the hugely stacked sponge cake layered with strawberries and cream. 'What is it?'

'Strawberry cassata cake—ricotta, whipped cream, Chambord, sponge and strawberries. That's what I've been searching for. What more could a girl possibly need?'

He laughed. 'I could be quite insulted by that.' He glanced back at the cake. 'Instead, I think I'll just order two.'

They sat at a table just across from the monuments and ordered the cake and two cappuccinos. One taste was enough. She was right. It was delicious.

'How on earth did you find out about this?' He was trying hard not to stare as she licked her fork.

'They had it at a café in London. Addison told me when I got to Italy I had to try the real thing.' She leaned back in her chair and looked first at the view and then at Reuben. She sighed. 'I think I'm in heaven.'

There was something about the way she said it that made his heart swell. It was absurd. It didn't matter that she'd been looking at him while she'd said it. He knew that she was talking about the whole experience. Was it wrong that he hoped she considered him part of it?

Four hours later, Lara was slumped against him as they walked slowly back to the bus. Today was officially the hottest day Italy had experienced in years. And every part of their bodies felt it. 'I can't believe my phone is full,' she grumped, her hat crushed beneath her fingers. She'd given up wearing it on her head, claiming it made her sweaty, and had started using it as an impromptu fan instead. Both of them agreed it was entirely useless.

Reuben pulled his T-shirt away from his back for about the tenth time that afternoon. They'd walked around the cathedral, the Baptistery and climbed the two hundred and ninety-seven steps to the top floor of the Leaning Tower. Lara had almost wept when they'd reached the top as, although the cathedral and Baptistery had been cooler, outside on the tower the heat was scorching. Their tour guide's joke about frying an egg on the pavement had been met with hard, exhausted stares.

'When we get back I'm going for a sleep,' Lara said, her head still resting on his shoulder.

'Me too,' he agreed. He could hardly believe he was used to working sixteen-hour days and yet a tour of Pisa had just about finished him. It didn't matter that there was something oddly comforting about having Lara slumped against him. She just seemed to fit so well.

He closed his eyes and it seemed like only a few seconds later that the tour guide was brushing against his arm. 'Wakey-wakey, everyone, we're back at the ship.'

Reuben stretched his back and stood up, holding out his hand towards Lara. Maybe it was time to have a conversation about what happened when they got back? They'd danced around the subject a few times. But after today's recognition about how he felt, maybe it was time to find out if his feelings were reciprocated. His stomach did a few flip-flops. The scary thing for him? Right now, he felt about as far away from his bad-boy reputation as humanly possible. There was a gorgeous woman only a few inches away who could potentially mash up his heart like modelling clay. Was he really brave enough to find out if she would?

He touched her shoulder and gave her a shake. 'Come on, Sleeping Beauty. We need to decide if we want to go to the theatre after dinner or just go for a few drinks.'

Her eyelids flickered open, revealing her blue eyes— a perfect match to the Mediterranean. He leaned forward a little. 'Maybe you should wear that blue dress tonight? It looked gorgeous and you haven't had a chance to show it off.'

Something caught his attention from the corner of his eye. The two elderly ladies from the cruise ship—Doris and Daisy. Doris's voice was getting louder and her actions more frantic as she tried to wake her counterpart. 'Daisy? Daisy? What's wrong? It's time to wake up. We're back at the ship now. Come on.'

Reuben didn't hesitate. He took a few steps closer. He was no doctor—he'd had no medical training at all—but that didn't mean he couldn't help. Daisy's colour was terrible, she was ashen and slumped to one side.

He touched Doris's arm. 'Why don't you go forward and speak to the coach driver?' He could see the pink of Lara's dress at his side. 'Lara will go with you and get some help. Let me sit next to Daisy for a few minutes.'

He glanced towards Lara, giving her all the information she could possibly need. Her lips pressed together as he almost lifted Doris from the seat and steered her forward. Lara took his place easily as he slipped into the seat next to Daisy.

He took a deep breath. He'd watched enough movies to know what he should do. They were right next to the cruise ship. Someone from the medical team would be here in moments. He put his fingers gently at Doris's wrist to feel for a pulse and watched her chest for any rise and fall. He felt a minor second of panic until he adjusted the position of his fingers and felt a rapid fluttering pulse. There was no way he could count that.

Doris's chest was rising and falling very slowly. Her pulse was fast and her breaths slow—what on earth did that mean? Reuben didn't have a clue. Her lips were tinged blue so he repositioned her slumped head, hoping her airway would be a little clearer and started to talk to her softly. 'Hi, Doris. It's Reuben here. I don't think you're feeling too good but don't worry. Daisy has gone to get some help.' He slid his hand into hers. 'It's been a really warm day. Maybe the heat just got a little too much for you? Whatever it is, don't panic. Help will be here soon. If you can hear me at all, give my hand a little squeeze.'

The rest of the passengers were filing off the bus, casting a few anxious glances in his direction. He sent up a silent prayer that one of them would be a doctor or nurse and offer to help. But it seemed like everyone was in the same boat as him. No medical expertise at all.

He could see some commotion on the dockside. Lara was talking anxiously to someone who was nodding and talking into a radio.

He kept his voice low and steady, sliding his other hand over to reassure himself she did actually still have the rapid pulse. Poor Daisy. The two old ladies had kept them entertained for days—even though he and Lara had been the butt of most of their jokes. The last thing he wanted was for something bad to happen.

A few minutes later the white-uniformed ship's doctor appeared with a whole host of equipment. Reuben was relieved to slide out of the way—and, when asked to assist carry Daisy in a stretcher a few minutes later—he was only too happy to help.

She was sped back to the ship on one of the golf-type buggies they used on the dockside.

Lara was standing outside the bus, waiting for him,

wringing her hands in front of her, lines of worry etching her face.

He slung his arm around her shoulder. 'Let's forget about the sleep. I need a drink and so do you. Something long and cold.'

She nodded and slipped her arm around his waist. 'Absolutely,' she agreed, as she watched the golf buggy pull up next to the ship.

Three hours later they'd found out that Daisy had suffered a mild case of sunstroke. She'd be monitored in the cruise medical centre overnight and even though they'd invited Doris to join them for dinner she'd insisted on staying with her friend.

Reuben was waiting in the sports bar for Lara. She'd asked him to give her a little time and space to get ready and he'd been happy to agree. He'd wanted to make a few calls to some of his clients and watch a Spanish football game to monitor another client.

It was odd how her stomach kept fluttering round and round. They'd already spent ten nights on this cruise ship. Ten nights sleeping in the same cabin.

But tonight felt different. Their relationship was changing. It was beginning to actually look like a relationship as opposed to two strangers just sharing a room. And she wasn't quite sure what that meant.

She put the finishing touches to her lipstick and hung some dangly earrings from her ears. Done. She opened the wardrobe door for a quick check in the full-length mirror, putting her hands on her hips and swinging from side to side.

The electric-blue dress was gorgeous. The slinky material hugged her skin without clinging, the fuller skirt swinging out as she moved from side to side. The wraparound style suited her. The tiny beads around the

V-shaped neckline caught the light as she moved in her silver sandals.

She picked up her silver bag and headed to the door. The ship was busy tonight, with more passengers having boarded in Livorno. She threaded her way through the crowd to the sports bar. It was packed. It seemed that every male on the ship had headed here to watch the game between two of the main Spanish football clubs. She spotted Reuben easily. He was sitting—no, almost standing—on a bar stool next to the main bar, his eyes fixed on a big screen. A deafening roar erupted around her as one of the teams scored and Reuben punched the air.

She couldn't hide her smile as she started to weave her way through the crowd.

It was hard to ignore the appreciative stares around her. It gave her confidence, confidence that had disappeared in the weeks since Josh had cheated on her.

She loved this holiday. She loved this ship. And she loved being in Reuben's company. He'd helped her realise that none of this was down to her. When she allowed herself to think back she knew things would never have worked with Josh. With hindsight, it was obvious he'd been using her. And even though she hated acknowledging it, she had to in order to move forward.

And that was exactly how she felt now—as if she was moving forward.

Reuben was wearing a pale blue shirt and dark trousers. She could see the outline of his muscles and defined waist beneath the fine fabric of his shirt. He'd caught her gaze and was watching her weave her way through the crowd. And this time there was something different in his look. It had always been there—simmering just beneath the surface—but now his gaze was full of pure unadulterated lust.

Her stomach muscles clenched and she could feel her

heartbeat starting to quicken. His eyes seemed to caress her as she moved towards him, skimming the way the dress clung to her curves. She lifted her chin, enjoying his gaze.

His brown eyes met hers. Unspoken words passed between them. None of this had been a figment of her imagination. Reuben Tyler, sports agents and a man with an income she couldn't even comprehend, was interested in her, Lara Callaway, nanny.

In any other lifetime she wouldn't have believed it.

But she wasn't interested in Reuben Tyler, sports agent.

She was interested in Reuben Tyler, the guy with a sexy accent that made her knees tremble and who was happy to eat cake and drink coffee with her. The guy had even taken her shopping—she hadn't met a guy like that before.

And she didn't have a fancy job title. She didn't even have anywhere to stay right now. And he certainly wasn't after her for her money. Here's hoping he just liked her for herself.

Her footsteps faltered, even though the floor was smooth and even. Recognition dawned in her. She'd been annoyed by Reuben's questions before. But he'd asked her the things she should have asked herself. She loved working for Addison and Caleb. She loved looking after Tristan. But was it really the job of her dreams, or had she just temporarily landed on her feet?

A tiny little part of her had always wanted to go back to university. She had the qualifications—all she had to do was reapply and save some money. She could do that. She could. Her footsteps started again with renewed confidence. Part of her felt guilty. She'd have to tell Addison her plans, and Addison had been good to her. But in a few years Tristan would be grown and wouldn't need her any more. He was due to start school after the summer. Her role would be reduced. It made sense to plan ahead now.

Reuben's brow had creased as her steps had slowed but now she gave him another smile. A smile of assurance. A smile of determination.

The momentum of her footsteps carried her onward, even though her stomach was still clenching a little. Confidence was a wonderful thing. But it could also be a curse.

She knew the attraction between her and Reuben was off the charts. But what next? She didn't want to be the next girl he was photographed with in the press. She wasn't interested in a fling or short-term thing. She wanted to be good enough for Reuben on a permanent basis. Not just a temporary one.

And tonight that's what she intended to find out.

CHAPTER ELEVEN

REUBEN HAD LOST all interest in the football game the second he'd spotted Lara across the room. It was impossible—he knew it but it was almost as if he could spot her sparkling blue eyes from the doorway and kept fixed on them as she moved towards him.

He didn't want to miss a single moment. The dress was perfect, hugging her curves and giving more than a hint of what lay beneath.

He sucked in a breath as for a few seconds her footsteps faltered. But it was only temporary. She met his gaze again and took the final steps towards him, coming closer than he would ever have expected, placing her hands firmly on his chest.

'So, what about this dinner, then?'

It was so direct. Straight to the point. And every cell in his body loved that.

But there was still that tiny part of him that was holding back. He liked this woman so much that he didn't want to do anything to hurt her. The surge of hormones was overwhelming. And they all gave one clear, direct message. Those blue, unblinking eyes were staring straight into his soul. Asking the question *What is this?* all over again.

Was he really brave enough to answer?

Her eyes were bewitching. Pulling him in. Making him feel as if things were really out of his control. Their flirtation had been going on from that first direct hit over his head. From the second he'd had his first view of the giant pink teddy bear. But that teddy bear had morphed into a real-life siren.

A siren that he couldn't even have imagined. Couldn't even have dreamed of.

He licked his lips and she unconsciously mimicked his act. He bent a little lower—more for him than for her. Now he could suck in her scent—the smell of shampoo, floral perfume and soap. Delicious. Now he could brush his lips against her ear and push back her silky soft hair. 'We've got seven to choose from. Which would you like to try?'

She turned her head slightly and fixed him with her gaze. 'Surprise me.'

There was a rush of blood around his body and a roaring in his ears. There was no way he could last the night. It was inevitable. Things had been building to this point from the very first moment. Tonight they were heading straight into the eye of the storm—straight into the climax.

He crooked his elbow towards her. 'Well, Ms Callaway, let's see where the night takes us.'

She raised her eyebrows as she tucked her arm into his elbow. 'Let's see indeed.'

They finally decided on the French restaurant. It had a quiet ambience with candlelit tables and a view of the ocean, a pianist on a grand piano in the corner and waiters who seemed to move without making a sound.

The plates of succulent food appeared and disappeared like moves in a carefully choreographed dance. She hardly tasted a thing. All she could think about was the main event.

Reuben appeared much calmer than she was. He spent the evening specialising in small talk, asking about her job, her plans and if she'd heard anything from the agent in London trying to find her a flat.

She'd almost forgotten about that.

She stared down at the trio of desserts in front of her. Every one of them she loved. But her stomach was too busy doing flip-flops to eat. 'I'll need to email her back. I'll do it tomorrow. I'm sure she's found me somewhere.'

'Hasn't she already sent you an email with some rentals?'

Lara sighed. 'Yeah, but one was too far away, another way too expensive and the other one was a shared flat with three other people. I'm not sure about that one.'

He gave a wicked smile. 'Are you worried they'll complain about your snoring?'

'What?' She flung her napkin towards him. 'I do not snore.' Then she stopped to think for a second and leaned forward. How would she know? 'At least, I don't think I do. Do I?'

The thought of Reuben listening to her snoring for the last ten nights filled her with complete dread.

He laughed and tossed her napkin back. 'Of course you don't.' He winked. 'I would have woken you up if you did.'

She tilted her head to the side. 'You talk in your sleep, you know.'

His eyes widened. He actually looked shocked. 'What?'

She smiled. 'Yeah, you do. Quite a lot, actually. Sometimes you have full conversations as if you're really talking to someone.'

He shifted in his seat and she couldn't help but feel amused at Reuben looking a little sheepish. 'What do I say?'

She gave a wicked smile and lifted her wine glass. 'Lots of things you probably shouldn't.'

He shifted again. 'I'm not sure I like the sound of that.' There was a rasp in his voice. It sent tiny tremors down her spine. Her imagination was working overtime.

She looked at him carefully. She didn't want to do anything to spoil the chemistry between them—but it was time to get it out there.

'You mutter mainly. Sometimes about your mum and dad, sometimes about Caleb.'

It was as if he froze. His hand was midway to his glass and it just stopped.

'Oh.'

'Oh? Is that all I'm going to get?'

His eyes were fixed on the table. For the first time all night he wasn't looking at her. It didn't feel right. It didn't feel natural. Eventually he ran his hand through his hair with a sigh.

He lifted his brown eyes to meet hers. 'I might not have been entirely truthful about why Addison doesn't like me much.'

It was like a little cool breeze over her skin. She set down her wine glass. 'Tell me.'

He stared out of the window at the gorgeous view. 'Addison came in at the wrong moment. Caleb had just called me on my behaviour.'

'What kind of behaviour?'

'He knew my parents. He knew what they were like. I was being childish. He'd told me he loved Addison and was going to marry her and I told him that love didn't exist and he was wasting his time on some fantasy.'

She wasn't sure where this was going. 'And?'

He sighed again. 'And, then he told me to grow up. He told me every kind of relationship wasn't like my mum and dad's. The world was full of people who loved each other just as much as he loved Addison and not to judge their relationship by the warped one my parents had.'

She pressed her lips together. 'Tough words.'

He gave the slightest shake of his head. 'Not really. They were all true. But I lashed out—I punched him— just as Addison walked through the door.'

Her hand went up automatically her mouth. 'Oh, no.'

He gave a sorry kind of smile. 'Oh, yes. Bad boy through

and through. No wonder she doesn't like me. I think she can't believe Caleb and I are still friends ten years later.'

Lara shook her head. There was something about the way he'd said the words. 'You're not all bad,' she said quietly, as she reached across the table and squeezed his hand.

His brown eyes fixed on hers. She lifted up her other hand. 'Look what you've done. Look what you've done for me.' She gave him a little smile. 'You've broken my run of loser boyfriends.' She laughed. 'And that's been going for my entire life. That's quite a feat, you know.'

He turned her hand over and started to trace little circles in her palm. 'I'm sorry, Lara. You've no idea how much I like you. I've never told anyone about my parents before—I've never told anyone about my fight with Caleb before. But with you? It's just easy. It's just as if it's meant to happen.'

Their gazes connected again. It was like a little zing in the air.

It's meant to happen.

She took a deep breath. 'You've given me confidence again, Reuben. Confidence I haven't had since I was a fifteen-year-old girl. You've made me question myself. You've made me question my potential and whether I'm doing what I really want to. I needed that. I needed that *so* badly. So thank you.'

His fingers stopped tracing the circles. 'What happens now?'

She licked her lips. 'Now we do what we're supposed to.'

He signalled to the waiter that they were finished and stood up. It was kind of hard not to stare at the part of his body that was right in front of her. But he seemed to be reading her mind, because he caught her hand and pulled her close to him.

Close enough to get the full effect.

She gulped. There was no chance of misunderstanding.

One hand splayed across her back, the other stroked a finger down her cheek. 'Want to go see the show?'

She shook her head. 'I think we should make our own show,' she whispered.

Her heart was clamouring inside her chest. She was conscious of the fact that every time she inhaled her breasts brushed against him. Conscious of the fact his eyes were fixed entirely on hers.

A tiny little part of her brain was screaming, *If you wanted to capture the bad boy, you've got him.*

She ignored every red flag that tried to raise itself above the parapet. For the first time in the last few weeks she felt entirely in control.

She felt confident in herself and her actions.

She didn't expect this to go anywhere. She had no expectations except for the here and now. She'd never thought like that before. But if she put up walls around herself then when Reuben walked away she'd be protected.

She slid her hand around his waist and grabbed his bum. This power thing was intoxicating. 'Shall we?'

The walk to the cabin had never felt so short. When she fumbled with the card Reuben's hand closed over hers, his breath at the back of her neck.

His voice was low, throaty. 'Lara, are you sure about this?'

The door clicked open and she spun to face him.

He'd never looked more handsome. Those dark brown eyes were pulling her into a warm chocolate oblivion. She reached up and ran her fingers through his hair, tugging him towards her.

'I've never been surer.'

CHAPTER TWELVE

REUBEN WAS DRUNK. Drunk entirely on Lara Callaway. She was like an infectious disease. A drug. And at some point he would tell her how he actually felt.

Just not right now.

Right now he'd just watch her sleep and wonder how on earth to play things when she woke up.

Because he should say something—shouldn't he?

He should talk to her about her job. About finding somewhere to stay. He could offer that she come and stay with him—it's not like he didn't have the room.

But it was almost as if something was stopping his tongue from functioning. It was the weirdest thing in the world. Every time he tried to imagine himself in a different place from where he was now he just couldn't see it. Couldn't see himself as part of the partnership. Couldn't see himself in a loving, reciprocal relationship.

It was ridiculous. He was adult enough to know that he was capable of whatever he wanted to be. But there were still those ingrained memories from childhood—and even now his reluctance to visit his family home. His associations of family were different from other people's. He hadn't realised how much it had scarred him.

He winced at the thought. He wasn't the type of guy to admit that anything scarred him. In lots of ways he'd been lucky. He'd had a roof over his head, clothes on his back and parents who did seem to care—in some part—about him. They just didn't care about each other.

Lara sighed in her sleep and turned towards him, one hand tucked under the pillow, the other reaching out towards him.

Lara had always had this crazy idea that she wasn't good enough. But it wasn't her that wasn't good enough— it was him.

A horrible cold sensation swept his body. What if he turned out like his dad? What if after a few years all they did was fight? And what if they brought kids into the equation and exposed them to same relationship he'd witnessed between his mum and dad?

That really made him feel sick.

Just as all these thoughts jumbled around his head Lara's eyes flickered open, those perfect blue eyes the same shade as the Mediterranean Sea outside.

She gave a lazy smile. 'Hey,' she whispered.

'Hey,' he replied. But it didn't come out quite right. Hers was sexy and content. His was terse.

A frown creased her brow and she leaned her head on her hand. 'What's wrong with you?'

'There's nothing wrong with me. I'm just not so sure this was the best idea.' *Where had that come from?* Sometimes his brain and mouth were completely detached from one another.

Something flickered across her face as she sat up in the bed and pulled the sheet up over her naked body. It was too late. He'd hurt her already. 'Well, it's a bit too late for that.' Her voice was matter-of-fact then she gave her head a little shake as if she couldn't believe what she was hearing. 'What is this—the morning after the night before?'

He winced. That made him feel terrible. He got out of bed—trying to get a little distance—and pulled on his jeans. 'Don't you have regrets?' The words were out before he really thought about them.

She hesitated for the tiniest second. 'No, not really. I

didn't think you'd propose marriage the next day, but at the least I hoped we'd still be friends.'

She'd hesitated. It didn't matter that he was the person who'd started this. It didn't matter that all of these insecurities were his, not hers. Now the only thing he could focus on was the fact she'd hesitated for the tiniest second when he'd asked her if she had regrets.

Lara shook her head, her hair fanning out around her shoulders. 'What's the problem? We're both adults. Look at us. It was inevitable that this was going to happen. We've been dancing around each other for the last few weeks.'

'And now we're not.' His response was automatic.

She halted.

He hated himself. He could almost see the shutters close across her eyes. He'd been too abrupt. He wasn't good at this kind of thing. Which was probably why he never got himself into these situations. His whole objective this morning had been to make sure he didn't hurt Lara and he'd completely blown that out of the water. He couldn't have made more of a mess of this if he'd tried.

It was just the words. They were jumbling around in his head. He couldn't think straight. He couldn't say what he really wanted to say.

He couldn't tell her that he thought he'd fallen in love with her and wanted her to be around permanently.

She stood up, wrapping herself in the sheet, and crossed to stand directly under his nose. 'What is this, Reuben?'

He pulled a T-shirt over his head. 'What's what?' he snapped. He couldn't help it. She'd already called him on this before. He'd hoped if it ever happened again he would be better prepared. Have an answer at his disposal.

If she'd asked him last night during dinner he would have told her it could be exactly what they wanted it to be.

So why couldn't he do that now?

Why were all his defences in place and every cell in his body telling him to get out of there?

Lara's face was an open book. He could see her confusion. He could see her hurt. He could see the pain in her eyes that he had caused.

His hand reached up automatically to touch her face but her body jerked away from him.

This was why he shouldn't do this. This was why relationships didn't work for him.

'You haven't answered me.' Her voice was shaking.

He hated the way his insides were twisting. Part of him wanted to congratulate her on her persistent questioning and the determined angle of her jaw.

He looked into her eyes. *This* was where he should tell her that he loved her. *This* was where he should tell her he wanted to spend the rest of his life with her.

This was where he should tell her that he was just being stupid. He was letting childhood experiences colour his adult life. But the words just wouldn't come.

He hated himself. And from the look on Lara's face she hated him too.

She pressed her finger to his chest. 'Why can't you let anyone in? Are you so damaged from your childhood that you can't let yourself love anyone just a little—or even try?' She was shouting now, furious with him. 'I thought you were an adult. I thought you said you'd put all that behind you—cut the toxic people out of your life. You know what people who love each other look like—you've seen Addison and Caleb. You know what things can be like if you'll only give them a chance.'

He couldn't speak. He was frozen. He could see the fury on her face and hear all the hurt in her voice, but he just couldn't reach out. He just couldn't take that step.

'Get out of my cabin, Reuben,' she said quietly.

And in the worst example of bad boy ever, he picked up his jacket and left.

Lara couldn't breathe. It was as if her lungs couldn't pull in any air. It didn't matter that she was only dressed in a sheet. Her head felt fuzzy and her legs weak as she yanked open the door to the balcony.

The warm outside air hit her immediately. She wasn't sure if it was better or worse. She leaned over the balcony, trying to suck in deep breaths.

After a few minutes her heart stopped clamouring against her chest and her head started to clear.

Still wrapped in the sheet, she took a few steps back. A few people down on the dockside were already staring up at her. She leaned against one of the glass doors.

Nightmare. Absolute nightmare.

She'd gone from the perfect night to the worst morning possible.

But the thing that hurt most hadn't been the look of confusion in his eyes, or the fact he'd more or less rejected her this morning. It was how she felt inside.

That little glimmer of confidence that had been seeded inside her since she'd first met Reuben had bloomed and grown. It had made her look at herself, realise she was worthy and make her look at the decisions she made in this life.

She wouldn't let him take that away from her. Not now. Not when she'd just got it back.

She stepped back inside the suite and stared around. She knew exactly what she needed to do.

Money didn't matter any more. She could easily put a flight on her credit card.

For her, this dream cruise was over.

It was time to get back to reality and make the changes she wanted and deserved.

She *was* worthy. And now she believed it.

But first she would see the Colosseum.

CHAPTER THIRTEEN

REUBEN HAD NO idea what he was doing. He had no idea where he was going. He just kept walking. It was amazing how far you could actually walk on a cruise ship.

He needed to clear his head. Everything he needed to say to Lara was actually in there. But from the way his heart was currently squeezing in his chest he would be lucky if he could ever form words again.

He stopped and leaned over the deck railing, trying to breathe in some fresh air. The ship had docked in Civitavecchia for Rome. His heart sunk.

This should be a great day. Lara had raved about visiting Rome. She'd been so looking forward to touring the city and visiting the Colosseum—they'd already signed up for the trips. Another black mark against his name.

He had to sort this out. He had to. In his working life he never had problems speaking his mind and putting things straight.

It was only his personal life that was such a screw-up. Trouble was, he'd never met anyone like Lara before. He'd never considered a long-term relationship. He'd never had one.

He stepped back from the railing and started walking again. His brain was spinning the whole time, trying to formulate an answer to the question, *What is this?* At this point an answer would not be enough. What he really needed was an answer followed by a heartfelt apology and whatever it would take to persuade her to give him a chance.

He kept walking. And walking. And walking.

The corridors of the ships were like a maze. All similar, with no real sense of direction. Eventually he came upon a sign: 'Medical Centre'.

Doris. Of course. He took five minutes to check and see how she was doing.

'Where's Lara?' she enquired.

He waved his hand and tried to brush off the remark. 'She's fine. She's getting changed. I'm sure she'll come and see you later.'

Doris gave him a careful look. It was almost as if she were looking directly into his brain and not liking what she was seeing. 'Okay, then,' she said stiffly.

He left. He had to. He had too much else to think about.

If he didn't get a grip he would lose Lara completely. Someone else would get her—with her pink teddy-bear suit, quirky sense of humour and giant blue eyes. Someone else would get to wake up next to her every morning. Someone else would get to hear about how her day had gone and get to feel the touch of those lips against theirs.

What could he offer?

Lara wasn't interested in the money or the celebrity. Lara was interested in *him*.

Probably more than he was interested in himself.

What did he really have to offer her?

Could he say those all-important words and tell her that he loved her? Because he couldn't last night. And he couldn't this morning.

They'd stuck in his throat.

And Lara had challenged him. She'd asked him again what this was.

She wasn't stupid. She was trying to sort out things

for herself, as much as for him. She'd been hurt already. Didn't need to be hurt again.

He had to leave.

The thought came like a blinding flash. If he couldn't find the words then he wasn't worthy of the relationship.

He wasn't worthy of Lara.

Caleb had told him grow up. It was finally time.

This wasn't the fairy-tale dream cruise he'd thought it would be. It had exposed him to feelings and emotions he hadn't expected.

He'd never connected to another person the way he'd connected to Lara.

And the truth was—he just didn't know what came next.

And now he'd hurt her.

The same look that he'd seen in her eyes when she'd spoken about Josh was now there when she looked at him.

The irony of her thinking she'd got away from loser boyfriends made him cringe.

Turned out Reuben Tyler was the biggest loser of them all.

All relationships weren't like the one his parents had. He was old enough, and had seen enough of life, to know it. So why did he let it still hold him back? He pushed the thought from his mind.

His feet started walking. He could leave. He could leave right now and let her enjoy the last few days of the cruise without him.

That was for the best.

That was exactly what he should do.

His legs powered him towards the suite. His brain was spinning. How would be explain he was leaving?

The door of the suite was ajar. He pushed it wide open.

The whole room was in disarray. The drawers were open and coat hangers were on the floor and on the bed.

He looked in the corner for her case. Gone.

He opened the door to the bathroom. All her items that had littered the little shelf below the mirror and driven him crazy had vanished.

There wasn't a single trace of her left.

Lara Callaway had bested him once again.

CHAPTER FOURTEEN

'I'VE HAD IT with you. I've had it with you and your bad attitude. You've let your team down, let the fans down and you've let your family down. Finally, you need to worry about the fact you've let me down. I'm done with you. I won't represent someone who thinks it's okay to treat other people with such disrespect. The club has sacked you and I won't be finding you another. This is finished. Find another agent.'

Reuben put down the phone. The rage was bubbling just beneath the surface but he'd managed to contain it. Coming home to the story that his client had punched a toilet attendant, groped some woman in the street and reneged on a visit to a children's hospital because he 'couldn't be bothered' had been enough for him.

And it was like a huge weight off his shoulders.

His secretary motioned to him through the glass. He walked outside and she handed him a brown paper package. 'Special delivery arrived for you. Want me to open it?'

Something squeezed around his heart.

He knew exactly what this would be.

'No. It's fine. Thank you.'

He walked back through to his office in The Shard and stared down at the city below.

He couldn't explain how it had been since he'd got back. He'd just felt…empty.

And he knew exactly why.

A figure on the street caught his eye. A woman with

blonde hair, jeans and brown leather boots. It couldn't be, could it? She was striding down the street with confidence, nodding to people as they passed.

She looked up as she reached the end of the street and broke into a run. A kind of strangled sound came out of his throat as she leapt up into the arms of a tall guy, putting her legs around him and clinging around his neck.

It wasn't Lara. Of course it wasn't Lara.

But it could be.

The wave of emotions that swept over him took what little breath he had left.

Caleb had been so right. It was time to put the past behind him. It was time to start living again.

He'd been a fool. He should have just grabbed hold of her with both hands and told her he wanted to give this a shot. He should have told her that from that first look she'd wound her way into his heart and his brain.

He should have told her he could spend the rest of his life watching her sleep, with her blonde hair splayed around her and the sun kissing her skin.

He should have told her that he loved her.

He watched the couple beneath him start to kiss passionately and his heart twisted in his chest.

That's what he was missing out on.

That's what he could have.

He picked up the parcel from his desk. The time to tell her that he loved her was now.

He could only hope and pray that she'd listen.

Lara looked out of the window onto the London street. It had been raining solidly since she'd got back. Her phone had been permanently switched off and all the messages on the house phone had naturally been for Addison and Caleb.

Her mood felt as wet as the weather.

Addison had left her a message, saying they'd be back a few days later. There had been no explanation and Lara was a little curious. It wasn't like she'd anything else to do to fill her time.

She opened another window on the internet. Last night she'd listed all her fancy clothes to resell. When on earth would she get the chance to wear them again? But her finger had hovered over the 'sell' button for too long. She'd just been unable to press it. She'd never owned clothes like that before and likely wouldn't again. She might keep them for an extra few weeks.

All the other windows opened were wishful thinking. On a whim last night she'd pulled up the prospectus for the university she'd wanted to attend. The entrance requirements hadn't changed. She could still make the cut.

Then she pulled up another—and another. Degrees had changed in the last few years. She could study English and French, English and German, English and History, English and Philosophy, even English and Creative Writing or English and Media. The list was endless. She'd spent a long time considering the English and Egyptology degree. How interesting would that be?

All she had to do was fill out the form. It was silly. As a mature student her application would be looked at differently. She didn't need to start at the beginning of the academic year. She would be able to start midterm if she wanted.

Her fingers hovered above the keyboard again. The key question was—did she?

She had confidence now. Confidence that Reuben had helped instil in her. She bit her lip and selected the university she'd always dreamed of and the degree that looked best. After half an hour she pressed 'send'. Done.

A noise at the door startled her. She stood up swiftly and strode over to the door. A delivery guy handed her a thick envelope and asked her to sign for it. She did it without even thinking—she signed for parcels for Addison and Caleb all the time.

But this one was different. This one was addressed to her.

She tore open the envelope, tipped it up and a data stick fell into her hand.

What?

She peered inside the envelope again There was a small sticky note. She pulled it out. *Watch me.* That was all it said.

She frowned and walked back to her laptop. Her hand hesitated next to the port. What if this was one of those things with a funny virus—one that would read her bank accounts and empty them?

She gave a rueful smile. Good luck with that, then. She might have got there first.

She stuck the stick in and waited until a message appeared on the screen, asking her what to do next. It only took a few seconds to get it to play.

A video screen appeared in front of her.

She blinked. Reuben Tyler. No way. What in the world…?

He held up a few pieces of white card with black writing, one after the other.

Her hand covered her mouth. She knew exactly what he was doing. He was imitating one of the films they'd watched together.

The words appeared quickly.

You might have guessed…
I'm not too good at this stuff…
You might even say…

I'm the worst in the world.
Words don't come easy to me...
And I'm afraid the ones that I do say...
Will be the wrong ones...
So I decided...
To get by...
With a little help from my friends.

She smiled at the song reference as he threw the last card away.

A few seconds later someone else sat down in front of the camera. It was a face she recognised instantly. Red Lennox, the baseball player Reuben represented.

He held one card in front of him.

What are we?

His trademark smile reached from side of his face to the other. It was clear he was highly amused by this. Her ears were flooded with his thick Texas accent.

'What are we? It's a good question—particularly for a man who is used to having all the answers. But it seems that he struggled with this one. So he asked for some help.'

Red held up a little piece of paper and held it front of him. He leaned towards the screen.

'Lara Callaway, I can't wait to meet you. It seems you're the one that got away. The one that he made a big mistake with.' His hands drew a wide circle in the air. 'Massive.' He winked at the camera. 'But it seems you are always on my mind.'

Red frowned at the card and glanced back at the camera.

'Should I be singing here?' He shook his head. 'I'm not sure. Anyway, it seems that Reuben wants to apologise, he wants to tell you that he knows exactly what you are.'

He leaned into the camera one more time and gave her a cheeky wink.

The camera picture faded out and in again. It was a different room. A different person sat down in the front of the camera.

Lara sucked in a breath. The tennis player Craig Robertson. He'd won Wimbledon twice. He was holding the white card too.

What are we?

Craig shook his head and shrugged his shoulders. 'I can't believe the guy who helped me propose to my girlfriend has made such a mess of things for himself. But here I am anyway. Anything to help a friend.'

He gave a smile.

'Love is a strange thing. I know. You don't realise it until it hits you over the head—or, in my case, throws you into a strange pool in France.'

He held up his hands.

'And then, when you do realise it's love, you're scared. Scared the other person won't feel the same way, scared you'll be out there on a limb. It can be hard to put it out there.' He winked at the camera too. 'But apparently some of us have a better gift of the blarney than others.'

Lara had stopped breathing. *Love.* These people were talking about love.

The tennis player tossed the card over his shoulder. 'Anyway, the point is, Reuben Tyler knows exactly what you are.'

The screen faded again. Another one?

Oh, yes. The billionaire footballer with the looks that had sold everyone in the world a bottle of aftershave. Dylan Bates. He had a card too.

What are we?

She let out her breath in one huge gasp. How on earth had Reuben managed this?

Dylan smiled. He was known across the planet as one of the nicest guys ever.

'It seems Reuben Tyler has just let the love of his life slip through his fingers because he couldn't find the right words. It's not that he didn't know them—he did. He just couldn't bring himself to say them. And now he feels like a total idiot.'

There was a huge twinkle in Dylan Bates's eyes. He leaned forward.

'I've waited a long time to see Reuben slayed by the love god, and it seems that it's finally happened. Lara Callaway, come and stay with me and my family in Los Angeles.' He tapped the side of his nose. 'I can give you lots of stories from years ago that you'll be able to use as blackmail material for years.'

He sat back.

'In the meantime, give him a chance. Everyone deserves a chance. Particularly this guy.' He held up his hands. 'What are we? You can bet Reuben Tyler knows.'

The screen faded to black.

Lara looked over her shoulder. It was almost as if she expected him to be standing there. That was it. Nothing else.

She looked back at the screen. Surely he would appear next and say something—anything?

But, no, the screen remained blank. She didn't know whether to laugh or cry.

For some reason her feet carried her to the door. She had no idea what she expected. Maybe the delivery guy would still be there with some other kind of message?

She yanked the door open and went to step outside. But her foot stopped midway. The step was blocked.

By a familiar shape dressed in a leather jacket and jeans. Beside him was a huge cake box. His head turned at the noise of the door opening.

Every little hair on her body stood on end, prickling her skin. Her breath caught in her throat. She left the door open and thudded down on the step next to him.

This was the oddest apology she'd ever had.

'Hey,' she said.

'Hey,' he replied. He gestured towards the box. 'I brought you a present.'

She gave a little nod and lifted the lid on the box. It was biggest strawberry cassata cake she'd ever seen. She tried not to smile. There was a spoon right next to it. She picked it up and dug right into the middle of the cake, pretending not to notice his eyebrows rising, and lifted a huge spoonful into her mouth. It was the real thing. She could almost hear the noise of the Piazza del Miracoli around her. She swallowed and waited a few seconds. It would take more than a cake to win her round. 'That was some video. Were you trying to tell me something?'

He threw back his head and laughed. 'You're not going to make this easy, are you?'

She gave a little smile. 'I think I'm going to make it as hard as possible.'

He shook his head. 'Call it like you see it. That's why I love you, Lara Callaway.'

Now she really couldn't speak.

'You what?' It was more of a squeak than anything else.

He turned on the step towards her, sucked in a breath and blew it out slowly through his lips. When his brown eyes fixed on hers she thought she would melt. 'It's kind of hard when you don't know what it is. It means when it hits you in the face like a wrecking ball you don't actually know what's happened.' The lilt in his accent sent shivers down her spine. It must get stronger the more emotional he was feeling.

She could see from his face how much he was struggling with all this. The easiest thing in the world would be to reach out and touch him. Run her fingers through his dark hair, feel his stubble under the palm of her hand.

But he still hadn't answered the question. And she really needed to hear him say it out loud.

'So, what happened, Reuben? What are we? I seem to have half the planet telling me that you know.'

He gave a nod and looked a bit rueful. 'I might have been a bit bad-tempered for a few days and some of my clients got together to bang my head on a brick wall.' He held up his hands. 'When I told them how much of a mess I'd made of things they were only too happy to tell me what they thought. I wasn't sure if you'd speak to me so I decided to ask them to help me out.'

'I think I just got the equivalent of a million-pound video clip.'

He sighed. 'I think it might have been a bit more.' His hand reached over slowly towards hers. 'I'm sorry, Lara. I'm sorry I didn't tell you exactly how I feel. I'm sorry I didn't tell you outside the casino in Monte Carlo that I loved you and thought you were the most beautiful woman that I'd ever seen.'

Tears prickled in the backs of her eyes. Finally, they were getting somewhere.

She lifted her gaze to meet his. 'Love can be a beautiful thing, Reuben. If you'll let it in.'

She let her words hang in the air between them. There was no need to say more. He knew exactly what she meant. He fumbled behind his back and pulled out a brown paper package.

It wasn't the most prestigious gift she'd ever seen. But it

charmed with its simplicity. The wrapping was uneven—
it seemed that Reuben had done this himself.

His hand closed over hers. 'I listened to what you said
to me. I've had a few days to think about it.' He handed
her the package.

She turned it over in her hands and released one of the
edges, sliding her hand inside to pull out the gift.

It wasn't what she'd expected. And part of her heart
skipped a few beats as the smile spread slowly across her
face. It was the most perfect, personal gift in the world.

'*Alice in Wonderland*! You found it. How did you do
that? It's exactly the same as the one I had when I was
a kid.'

His brown eyes fixed on hers as he smiled. 'I worked
out what year you were born and what edition you were
likely to have had.' He leaned forward and whispered into
her ear. 'I'll let you into a secret. I have another three in
case that was the wrong one.'

She ran her hand over the pale blue cover of the book.
'No. This is definitely the right one. It's perfect. Thank
you.'

He hesitated then pointed at the book. 'Open it.'

She took a deep breath and opened the hardback cover.
A silver key on a red ribbon was sitting on the first page.

'You told me I had to let people in. And I think you
were right.' He held up the key, 'So, this is how I start.
I'd like to let you in. I'd like to give us a chance. And this
is my way. A key to my house and a key to my heart.' He
gave a wary little smile that warmed her heart.

He was nervous. He was *really* nervous about this.
And this was what she loved. It didn't matter about his
bad-boy reputation. She knew the real Reuben Tyler. Not
the guy who was the hotshot agent. Not the guy who had
lots of money.

She knew the guy who'd practically had to bring himself up. The guy who'd had no real example of what love was. She knew the truly laid-bare Reuben Tyler—that was the guy she loved.

The key was dangling in the air. She reached out with an open palm and held it underneath. She had to push him just a little bit further. 'So, what does this mean, Reuben? What are we?'

It was the million-dollar question. The thing she really needed him to embrace.

She heard him suck in a breath. 'We're whatever we want to be, Lara.'

She still hadn't taken the key. She really wanted to just swoop in and grab it. But a little part of her heart needed a little more. She knew this was an enormous step for Reuben, but she didn't just want a little part of him—she wanted the whole thing. The real deal.

She tried her best to stop her voice from wobbling. 'And what do you want us to be?'

He turned to face her, dropping the key in the palm of her hand and putting both his hands on her face. 'I want us to be together. I want you to be the person I see first thing every day. I want you to be the person to tell me when I'm being cranky. I want you to be the person I share amazing sunrises and sunsets with all around the world. I want to know when I get off a plane I have the girl who's captured my heart to talk to, no matter where I am. I want to look forward to coming home to you. I want to feel as if I'm coming home because I've got a reason to come home. I've found the person I want to love for the rest of my life.' He stopped for a second, and she could tell he was trying to keep himself in check. His voice was beginning to waver.

Tears brimmed in her eyes. She didn't doubt that this was the most emotionally open Reuben had ever been.

And it was with her. Because he loved her—just like she loved him.

She reached up and covered one of his hands with hers. 'I have too.' She gave him a heartfelt smile. 'But we might have a few issues.'

A frown creased his brow. 'Why?'

She ran her fingers down the outside of his palm. 'Because you think you're getting a girl with a job as a nanny.'

She saw the little light of recognition flicker in his eyes. A smile hinted at his lips. 'What am I actually getting?'

She couldn't help her smile. 'You're getting the world's lousiest student. I'm going to have to learn a whole heap of new skills. And for that I'm going to need a guy who is patient, understanding and who can put up with takeaways, books spread everywhere, and lots of moans and groans at exam times.'

He pulled her into his arms. 'You've applied?'

She nodded. 'I've applied.'

His lips hovered next to hers. 'Well, I guess we've got that in common. I'm applying too. For a job that I've no idea if I'll be any good at—but I want to spend the rest of my life finding out.' He ran a finger down her cheek and stared into her eyes. She'd never loved him more. 'But I haven't found out yet if my application has been accepted. Thing is, I think the panel pretty's tough.' His lips brushed against hers.

She tried to respond instantly but he held himself just a few millimetres away, teasing her. 'When do you think I'll find out?'

She ran her hand down his chest. 'Oh, I think you can find out almost immediately. There's just one tiny little thing.'

'What's that?'

'Do I have to share the cake?'

Reuben threw back his head and laughed then captured her mouth with his. And as her fist closed around the shiny key in her palm she knew.

She knew this was the man she'd spend the rest of her life loving and she couldn't wait to start.

* * * * *

MILLS & BOON®
Hardback – January 2016

ROMANCE

The Queen's New Year Secret	Maisey Yates
Wearing the De Angelis Ring	Cathy Williams
The Cost of the Forbidden	Carol Marinelli
Mistress of His Revenge	Chantelle Shaw
Theseus Discovers His Heir	Michelle Smart
The Marriage He Must Keep	Dani Collins
Awakening the Ravensdale Heiress	Melanie Milburne
New Year at the Boss's Bidding	Rachael Thomas
His Princess of Convenience	Rebecca Winters
Holiday with the Millionaire	Scarlet Wilson
The Husband She'd Never Met	Barbara Hannay
Unlocking Her Boss's Heart	Christy McKellen
A Daddy for Baby Zoe?	Fiona Lowe
A Love Against All Odds	Emily Forbes
Her Playboy's Proposal	Kate Hardy
One Night...with Her Boss	Annie O'Neil
A Mother for His Adopted Son	Lynne Marshall
A Kiss to Change Her Life	Karin Baine
Twin Heirs to His Throne	Olivia Gates
A Baby for the Boss	Maureen Child

MILLS & BOON®
Large Print – January 2016

ROMANCE

The Greek Commands His Mistress	Lynne Graham
A Pawn in the Playboy's Game	Cathy Williams
Bound to the Warrior King	Maisey Yates
Her Nine Month Confession	Kim Lawrence
Traded to the Desert Sheikh	Caitlin Crews
A Bride Worth Millions	Chantelle Shaw
Vows of Revenge	Dani Collins
Reunited by a Baby Secret	Michelle Douglas
A Wedding for the Greek Tycoon	Rebecca Winters
Beauty & Her Billionaire Boss	Barbara Wallace
Newborn on Her Doorstep	Ellie Darkins

HISTORICAL

Marriage Made in Shame	Sophia James
Tarnished, Tempted and Tamed	Mary Brendan
Forbidden to the Duke	Liz Tyner
The Rebel Daughter	Lauri Robinson
Her Enemy Highlander	Nicole Locke

MEDICAL

Unlocking Her Surgeon's Heart	Fiona Lowe
Her Playboy's Secret	Tina Beckett
The Doctor She Left Behind	Scarlet Wilson
Taming Her Navy Doc	Amy Ruttan
A Promise...to a Proposal?	Kate Hardy
Her Family for Keeps	Molly Evans

MILLS & BOON®
Hardback – February 2016

ROMANCE

Leonetti's Housekeeper Bride	Lynne Graham
The Surprise De Angelis Baby	Cathy Williams
Castelli's Virgin Widow	Caitlin Crews
The Consequence He Must Claim	Dani Collins
Helios Crowns His Mistress	Michelle Smart
Illicit Night with the Greek	Susanna Carr
The Sheikh's Pregnant Prisoner	Tara Pammi
A Deal Sealed by Passion	Louise Fuller
Saved by the CEO	Barbara Wallace
Pregnant with a Royal Baby!	Susan Meier
A Deal to Mend Their Marriage	Michelle Douglas
Swept into the Rich Man's World	Katrina Cudmore
His Shock Valentine's Proposal	Amy Ruttan
Craving Her Ex-Army Doc	Amy Ruttan
The Man She Could Never Forget	Meredith Webber
The Nurse Who Stole His Heart	Alison Roberts
Her Holiday Miracle	Joanna Neil
Discovering Dr Riley	Annie Claydon
His Forever Family	Sarah M. Anderson
How to Sleep with the Boss	Janice Maynard

MILLS & BOON®
Large Print – February 2016

ROMANCE

Claimed for Makarov's Baby	Sharon Kendrick
An Heir Fit for a King	Abby Green
The Wedding Night Debt	Cathy Williams
Seducing His Enemy's Daughter	Annie West
Reunited for the Billionaire's Legacy	Jennifer Hayward
Hidden in the Sheikh's Harem	Michelle Conder
Resisting the Sicilian Playboy	Amanda Cinelli
Soldier, Hero...Husband?	Cara Colter
Falling for Mr December	Kate Hardy
The Baby Who Saved Christmas	Alison Roberts
A Proposal Worth Millions	Sophie Pembroke

HISTORICAL

Christian Seaton: Duke of Danger	Carole Mortimer
The Soldier's Rebel Lover	Marguerite Kaye
Return of Scandal's Son	Janice Preston
The Forgotten Daughter	Lauri Robinson
No Conventional Miss	Eleanor Webster

MEDICAL

Hot Doc from Her Past	Tina Beckett
Surgeons, Rivals...Lovers	Amalie Berlin
Best Friend to Perfect Bride	Jennifer Taylor
Resisting Her Rebel Doc	Joanna Neil
A Baby to Bind Them	Susanne Hampton
Doctor...to Duchess?	Annie O'Neil

MILLS & BOON®

Why shop at millsandboon.co.uk?

Each year, thousands of romance readers find their perfect read at millsandboon.co.uk. That's because we're passionate about bringing you the very best romantic fiction. Here are some of the advantages of shopping at www.millsandboon.co.uk:

* **Get new books first**—you'll be able to buy your favourite books one month before they hit the shops

* **Get exclusive discounts**—you'll also be able to buy our specially created monthly collections, with up to 50% off the RRP

* **Find your favourite authors**—latest news, interviews and new releases for all your favourite authors and series on our website, plus ideas for what to try next

* **Join in**—once you've bought your favourite books, don't forget to register with us to rate, review and join in the discussions

Visit **www.millsandboon.co.uk**
for all this and more today!